A LIFE BY DESIGN

DESIGN

(THE ITALIAN FAMILY SERIES)

Lucy Appadoo

This book is dedicated to my parents who have always supported me in my life journey. They have the biggest of hearts.

TABLE OF CONTENTS

CHAPTER 1
TWO MINDS

(September 1972)

Elena flicked open the envelope, her heart racing. Her fingers trembled as she slowly pulled out the piece of paper and unfolded it. Taking a deep breath, she closed her eyes and willed herself to take a peek. Was she ready? Had she got in? What if her dream was shattered? Only one way to find out.

Here goes. Summoning the courage, Elena glided her fingers over the letter and read the first few lines. It said, *"Congratulations! You have been accepted into Istituto Marangoni in Milan to study our Bachelor of Arts (Honours) in Fashion Design."*

Elena swallowed, her body frozen in shock. She had finally been accepted to study fashion design in Milan. That meant her days in Laurino were numbered and she'd get the chance to explore another part of the world. Her chance to move away from the family farm. Her time to leave her stifling part-time job at the clothes shop, where every day was just like the one before. Sometimes she thought another day in Laurino would kill her. But now she'd have the life she had always dreamed about.

Reading the rest of the letter, she felt a lightness over her body and drew a hand through her long, chestnut hair. Only recently, she had convinced her father to let her put crimson highlights into her hair, which had made her feel like an adult. At twenty years of age, Elena dreamed of bigger things than the village. She wanted to spread her wings and study what she loved. She loved reading anything, but she was most inspired by her love of fashion, and read all she could about it. Even her sister Valeria inspired her, sending letters describing the successful dressmaking business she'd started in Melbourne. Valeria had escaped, and now it was Elena's turn.

Elena watched the backs of her father, Enzo, who was drinking a glass of wine, and her mother Graziella huddling over the sink washing dishes. Their small kitchen featured an elongated table with a small bench space, and a wood fire oven. New pots and pans hung above the bench, replacing some rusty and old ones they'd had. The weathered crockery looked ready to be thrown out too, but their limited funds meant they would make do with the old and worn kitchenware. Her mother made the best of her equipment by cooking simple, yet tasty foods made with organic, home-grown vegetables from their farm.

Her father slouched at the table and flicked through the newspaper. He thumbed through the pages and turned to Elena with a curious stare when she cleared her throat. He laid the newspaper down and squinted. "What's with you, Elena?"

Somersaults in her stomach plagued her. She swallowed and wondered how to broach the subject of moving to Milan. Taking a full breath, Elena drew a shaky hand through her strands. "Mama, can you sit with us? I need to talk to you both."

Her mother turned off the faucet, wiped her hands on a tea towel, and sat at the table with a frown. "What's going on, dear?"

Elena picked up the letter and handed it to her father. She waited until he read it, his body flinching, and his mouth curling downward. He threw it over to her mother with a grunt. Her mother scanned it, then looked up at Elena with a worried glance.

Her father clenched his hands and shook his head. "There's no way in hell you're going to Milan. Not while I'm alive, you're not."

Elena flinched, but held his gaze. She knew she'd have a fight on her hands, but she wouldn't give up.

Her mother tilted her head. "Elena, this is far away. You're only twenty, and this is a place without anyone we know. How can we let you leave on your own?"

Elena braced herself. "Please, Mama. This is a chance of a lifetime. My dream. If I could study fashion in the village I would. But for me to have a real chance at a profession, I have to leave the village. There's a big wide world out there."

Her father smashed his hand against the table, sending a tremor through Elena's body. "Over my dead body! You are not going to Milan, and that's final. I'll hear nothing more about it."

"But, Papa, this is my dream." She pressed her hands against her sides to keep them from shaking. "This is the only place I can study. Can't you at least think about it? I am an adult now. You can't expect me to work on the farm or in the shop my whole life. Don't you want me to have a future?"

2

He glared. "You never once complained about your life here. This is just about Valeria leaving, but she had Roberto to marry, and we trusted his family. In Milan, you have no one. This is out of the question."

Elena's stomach clenched. "Papa, please. Just think about it!"

Veins popped out on his head. "Enough!" He stood up and stormed out of the house without a further word.

Elena turned towards her mother, who stared into the distance. Elena's voice seemed to draw her back. "Mama, can you please convince Papa. Please, Mama!"

Her mother clasped her hands together. She reread the letter, and tears streamed down her cheeks. With a wistful look at Elena, she said, "I don't want you to give up on your dreams, Elena, but I'm frightened for you. This is so far away from us, and you'll be on your own. How would we know you'd be safe?"

Elena leaned in. "I can ring you every day until you're sure I'm safe. Until I've made some friends. Please, Mama, think about it, and try to convince Papa. I still have time before I make a decision."

Her mother nodded. "Leave it with me, darling, but I cannot make any promises."

"That's all I ask."

At least now there was a semblance of hope.

CHAPTER 2
A HUGE FEAT

Two weeks had gone by, and during that time, Elena cajoled, sweet-talked, rationalised, and fought with her father over her study trip to Milan. He wouldn't budge, and she began to form a plan in her mind. She didn't want to be estranged from her family. There had to be a way for her father to agree to her leaving.

Her mother begged her father to reconsider, but to no avail. With each passing day, Elena's anxiety rose. How could she work in a clothes shop and on the farm for the next working years of her life? She feared she would fall ill if she kept thinking about her fate.

She was afraid her father would disown her if she left the village without his blessing. He might never let her see her mother again. Oh, sure, she could sneak around and see Mama, but that would make her mother's life that much harder, and Mama had suffered more than enough in her life. Elena didn't want to put any extra pressure on her mother when she could resolve this situation herself.

I can stay here, she thought, *or I can figure out a way to leave here respectfully and with my parents' blessing.*

There had to be a way to convince her father to agree.

She lay back against the sofa, watching her brother Emilio wander over and plonk himself down beside her. He knit his brows and spread out his hands as if she was giving him the evil eye. At eighteen, Emilio was handsome with his black crew-cut and his solid, muscular build. He always complained about his short height, but the girls flocked towards him in spite of that.

"What's going on, sister?"

She leaned forward and planted her hands under her chin, as a thought formed in her mind. "How would you like to go on a vacation, Emilio?"

Emilio drew back, his eyes widening. "Are you talking about Milan? Has Papa agreed for you to go yet?"

She shook her head. "Don't be silly. He's never going to let up. Unless you come with me. He seems to have these double standards, so I think if you tell him you'll be my chaperone, he might just let me go."

"I don't know." He scratched his temple. "I mean, what am I going to do in Milan? I've got my work on the farm here, and I don't mind doing that."

Elena rose from the sofa, paced the floor, and stood over her brother. "Just do this for me. Then once you've stayed awhile you can come back home. By that time, he'll have your report that I'm safe and have met people."

Emilio swung his left leg over his knee and squeezed his calf muscle. He seemed to be processing things, so she wouldn't rush him. He was always a deep thinker, an interesting trait in a man who loved to work with his hands. "So how are you going to pay for all this?"

Elena thought fondly of Giovanna. Who would have thought the cranky old woman from down the street would turn out to be such a friend to Elena's family? Their neighbour had felt such a strong sense of guilt after her son, Gregorio, had hurt Valeria that she'd left a portion of her estate to Valeria and her siblings. Since Valeria had refused any payment, the money had been divided among Elena, Emilio, and Carla. The only guilt Elena felt was that, because of Giovanna's gift, Gregorio and his two siblings, Aldo and Daniela, got a smaller portion.

She wasn't sure if they knew about it, and she hoped they didn't. Gregorio and Daniela attended Giovanna's funeral, but Aldo hadn't even sent his regards. The nerve of him. He'd taken his mother's money easily enough when she was alive, only to show a complete lack of respect when she'd died. At least Giovanna had her friends and other family in the village pay their respects. Even without Aldo, it was a memorable funeral.

Gregorio had spent quite a number of months in prison for what he'd put Valeria through, and word was, he was a changed man. He was openly despondent at his mother's funeral and showed warmth towards Elena's family. He had apologised profusely. But Elena still didn't trust him. What if it was an act? Maybe he hadn't changed at all. She hardly knew Daniela at all, even though she'd moved into her mother's home, refusing to sell Giovanna's house.

The euros that Giovanna had given Elena would be just enough for her studies, but she would need extra money for living expenses.

However, she might never travel to Milan if she couldn't convince her father, and soon. She had responded to the letter with interest and explained how she would need more time to possibly accept the offer, but time was running out.

"Earth to sister. Earth to sister." She came out of her reverie and looked up at Emilio. "How are you funding this trip?"

"Giovanna's money."

"It won't be enough. What about the rest?"

Elena's heart sank. She needed Emilio on her side. "I can get a part-time job while I'm studying."

"It's not that easy to get work in a strange city. You don't even know Milan and you don't have real experience."

Elena laughed. Her brother was wise to the world, but still immature in some ways. "I have my sales experience from the shop and I know how to work on a farm. I have useful skills, brother."

Before Emilio could respond, her parents entered the house and greeted them. Her father held a questioning look. He stood cross-armed, as if he knew what she was thinking. He knew her too well to think she'd give up that easily.

"Papa. I have an idea." She turned towards her brother. "Emilio can come with me to Milan, and then I won't be alone."

Her father squared his shoulders and pursed his lips. With a shake of the head, he said, "And here I thought Valeria was stubborn and independent. You are even more so. You'll be the death of me, Elena."

In spite of his words, she could tell he was fighting hard to hide a smile as her mother turned towards him.

"That's not a bad idea, Enzo. She wouldn't be alone. Then once she's settled and we know she's safe, Emilio can come back home. We all win."

Enzo's eyes narrowed. "Hmmm. Let me think about it."

CHAPTER 3
THE JOURNEY

Elena struggled to breathe as her sister Carla pulled her into a tight embrace. "Carla, I love you, but you're suffocating me."

Fiumicino Airport buzzed with tourists and locals rushing about with luggage. The sounds of squealing voices and loud announcements was almost deafening. Having come from a quiet village, she wasn't used to the noise and hectic pace.

Carla let go with a taut smile and looked down at her sister. "I am sorry, Elena. I will miss you just like I miss Valeria. Please keep in touch." She blinked back the tears and drew a shaky hand through her brown waves.

"And I'll miss you too." Elena turned to Carla's husband, Maurizio, and they embraced. "Take care of my sister or you'll have me to deal with."

Maurizio nodded. "It'll be my pleasure. You have a safe flight."

Elena smiled, thinking how lucky Carla was to have met a genuine and loving man who loved her with all his heart. They were happily married, and Elena had a feeling they'd be having babies soon.

Emilio hugged his mother, Carla, and Maurizio. Elena wondered why her father never showed the courage to say goodbye at the airport. He'd refused to see Valeria off at the airport when she had moved all the way to Australia, and now he was doing the same to Elena. She had said her goodbyes to him at home, and luckily for her, a few of her friends and her next-door neighbour, Maria, had visited her at home to say goodbye.

Elena's chest tightened at the sight of her mother. Her petite frame made her look almost fragile; in fact she was anything but. Her mother was a force to be reckoned with; a superwoman who could do no wrong, except for tolerating the dominance of her father. He had mellowed somewhat since Valeria had left for Australia, but Mama still had to fight for every little thing she'd wanted. He'd never made her life easy.

Her mother ran into her daughter's arms and stroked Elena's hair. When they pulled apart, her mother's cheeks were blotchy and damp with tears. She wiped her tears away and managed a smile.

"Please, darling Elena. You be safe. As soon as you get there, please ring Maria. She will call us quickly when you are on the phone."

Elena nodded. "I'll do that, Mama. Please don't worry. I'm a grown woman and will be fine. Don't go thinking the worst."

"Oh, darling, after what happened to Valeria and Dario, I always worry about you girls. Besides, it's a mother's job to worry."

Elena took a breath. "But Valeria's happy with Roberto. They have their beautiful daughter, so it all turned out well in the end."

Her mother rubbed at her tears. "It sure did."

Emilio gave her arm a quick tug, and they both rushed into the queue towards the tarmac. Elena turned away from her family, her body shaking at the memory of her family's saddened faces. She would most likely not see them for a few years, and, for a moment, she wondered if she was doing the right thing. Was she ready for this? She was only twenty years old and Emilio was eighteen, and they'd never ventured outside of their village of Laurino.

Yet Elena loved a challenge and adventures. She planned to write about her adventures one day, as she liked delving into creative writing. It was a hobby for now. Fashion design was her priority.

Once Elena and Emilio shuffled their way through to their allocated seats on the plane, Emilio held his sister's hand then kissed her on the cheek.

"Thanks, Elena, for this. I can't wait to see a new city. So exciting."

She chuckled. "If it wasn't for you, I wouldn't be going to Milan, so thanks, brother."

He settled back against his seat and closed his eyes. Elena looked straight ahead, watching passengers push their hand luggage into the overhead compartments. A chill crawled up her spine as she pondered the unknown in Milan. She kept thinking about needing to find a part-time job. Her parents had managed to collect money from their Italian community, so she had a bit of money to spend on incidentals and housing, but it wouldn't last long. The money that Giovanna had given her would only cover the course fees.

Luckily for her, a friend of her aunt's lived in Milan not too far from the fashion institute, so she and Emilio could stay there. She'd have to pay board, though, and help out around the house. It wouldn't be a free ride.

She was told stories about this woman she'd be living with, and they weren't very endearing. According to her aunt, her friend, Nunziata, was a widow and childless. Nunziata had a very strict routine and if Elena didn't abide by it, she'd be kicked out before she could say *fashion*. Elena swallowed. Surely, she could put up with a few strict rules after living her whole life with a domineering father. Couldn't she?

CHAPTER 4
SETTLING IN

Emilio and Elena disembarked from the plane, picked up their luggage, and made their way outside the Milan airport. A row of buses lined the kerb and crowds formed outside as others were assisted with their luggage onto the back of the bus.

Emilio glanced at his sister. She was pushing along her suitcase as if feeling the weight across her back. Emilio wrinkled his nose and wiped his brow. Smells of exhaust fumes and burning rubber penetrated his nose. They caught up to the line and waited behind other passengers who eventually made room for them at the front of the bus.

Emilio had the address of the woman they'd be staying with. He recited the address to the driver who looked at him with a bored expression.

"It's a fair walk from the bus stop." He gave Emilio directions.

Emilio thanked him and found a seat with Elena out front with her belongings. He felt a headache coming on as he waited for other passengers to enter until the bus drove off, jolting over bumps and passing out of the airport. The tall buildings and skyscrapers blinded him. He peered through the window and came across art and historical museums, galleries, theatres, universities, and towering monuments. It was such a busy and spectacular city.

He was in awe of the excitement and adventure coming his sister's way, but he would miss her once he left. He'd worry about her as well. She was naive in the ways of the world. An uneasy feeling chilled his body. Maybe Elena wasn't as resilient as she thought. Being in the village was different, but out here there were a lot of strange people, particularly strange men. She had to be extra diligent in who she trusted.

The bus eventually stopped in Lombardy. Emilio and Elena were the first to exit the bus while the other passengers trailed behind, knocking him in the back. He sighed as passengers pushed and prodded him towards the exit.

They heaved their luggage off the bus. He hoped they didn't have too far to walk to their new residence.

As they ambled their way to the set of apartments, he watched a man playing the guitar on a second-floor balcony. Potted plants lined the ground, and clothes hung over rickety railings. The timber-framed windows were weathered, and the concrete building was cracked and worn. Was this where they were going to live? He had a bad feeling about this, but he wouldn't jump to conclusions. Looks could be deceiving. At least they had a home and somewhere to settle, so he couldn't complain.

From what his mother had told them, he knew Nunziata lived on the bottom floor. He knocked on the heavy door and waited. Turning to Elena, he noticed her frown. She shrugged but said nothing.

A short, chubby woman with green eyes and grey hair set in a bun opened the door. She pursed her lips. Her eyes felt like they were boring into Emilio's soul. A cold feeling swept through him. He was worried for his sister.

"You must be Emilio and Elena. I'm Nunziata."

Elena put out her hand. "Pleased to meet you." The woman ignored the hand and swung the door further open.

"Well don't just stand there. Get in. I don't have all day."

Emilio swallowed and turned to Elena, whose face had turned beetroot red. It was only the afternoon, but he felt like it was going to be a long day.

"I'll show you to your rooms. You'll have to share as I don't have any other room."

Emilio looked around the foyer and found grimy bare walls, a huge pot filled with an artificial plant, a big statue of Jesus facing one of the rooms, and a clothes rack.

Nunziata opened the door to the room across from Jesus. Inside were two single beds, an armoire, a drawn window that seemed to filter in light, two gold-coloured lamps, and pictures of Jesus and Mother Mary above each of the beds. The room was medium-sized but tidy enough for their simple needs.

Nunziata turned to both of them, looking them up and down with a grunt. "Now, dinner is at 6.00pm sharp but every other night you'll be cooking your own food. I don't give any handouts." She took a breath. "And I expect you to do chores tomorrow. No questions."

Emilio put up his hand. "Any chance we could have a drink?"

11

The woman squinted at him. "If you must, I'll show you to the kitchen and you can grab one yourself. There's a jug of water in the fridge." She headed back the way they'd come, and Emilio followed. When he turned back to Elena, she looked on with a shake of her head.

Who was this woman? Why was she so rude and cold? It would be expected that after a long trip they'd want a drink. How would poor Elena ever cope living this way? He wasn't staying long, and then she'd be on her own. Elena was most likely leaving one prison for another. Was he leaving her in good hands?

CHAPTER 5
ACCLIMATISING

The next day, Elena woke up and stretched out her arms. Her back ached from the firm and lop-sided single mattress. She pulled herself up and rubbed her lower back with both hands. For a moment, she felt disoriented and wondered where she was. Oh yes, Nunziata's home. An unwelcoming bull-terrier with a tabby cat. At least she had somewhere to stay.

Over to the side, Emilio slept and snored loud enough to wake the dead. He tossed and turned but didn't wake up.

Elena yawned and swung her legs over the side of the bed. She bent down towards her suitcase and rummaged through clothes she didn't put away yesterday. Finally, settling on a peach dressing gown, Elena put it on and headed outside towards the kitchen. Nunziata sat at the table, eating a brioche with a minute cup of espresso. She looked up at Elena and nodded but didn't smile.

"If you want breakfast you'll need to do your own shopping." She rose, grabbed a piece of crumpled paper, and shoved it in Elena's hand. "Here you go."

Elena drew back. "What's this?"

"Details about nearby shops and the board you need to pay. I expect payment every week, and if it's a day late, you're out of here. I cannot afford lateness, and there are plenty of other students I can get to live here."

Elena was almost speechless. What was wrong with this woman? "Sure. I'll have it to you by the end of the week."

"Good." Nunziata looked towards the rusty fridge. "Now, just for today, if you want breakfast, I have a few eggs left, but make sure you replace them. You need to get your own oil and salt too. Remember, I don't give any handouts. I buy for me and you buy for yourself and your brother. Understand?"

Elena nodded with a sick feeling in her stomach. Some adventure this would be. She headed towards the fridge and grabbed an egg. She searched for a frying pan, opening and closing cupboards until she found a weathered stainless-steel pan. Nunziata got off her seat, drank down her coffee, placed the cup in the sink, and stormed out. Well, how rude. This woman knew that

Elena came from the village and that the city was a big change for her, but instead of helping her acclimate to her new home, Nunziata treated her like a piece of rubbish.

As Elena was frying an egg and spooning oil over the yolk, Emilio walked in and rubbed his eyes. He approached his sister and planted a kiss on her cheek. "Morning. How did you sleep?"

Elena turned to him. She set aside the egg onto a cracked plate. "Badly." She yawned. "Would you like an egg?"

"Sure." He sat down and looked around the kitchen. "Where's you know who?"

Elena whispered, "Probably on her broomstick."

Emilio chuckled. "That bad again, ha?"

Elena scooped up the egg and set it down onto a plate. Then she fried another egg and watched the oil sizzle in the pan. Placing it onto another plate, she handed it to Emilio, then grabbed cutlery from a drawer. No matter how she pushed and prodded the drawer, it wouldn't close properly. "Worse."

They sat together, eating their eggs in silence. Elena pondered her day's tasks. She still had a few weeks before starting her course, but settling into the place meant she needed to scour the area and buy clothes that suited her new role as a student.

"So, what's your plan for today?" Emilio asked.

"Shopping. I also need to get groceries for us. Do you want to come?"

"No, I'll be going out later. If you like, I can get the groceries and you can do your clothes shopping."

"Are you sure? You won't know what to buy."

"Just give me a list. Mama gave me some money."

Elena nodded. "Okay, I'll do that after I shower."

When she was dressed and the list safely in Emilio's pocket, she hurried out onto the street and wandered aimlessly until she found a bus stop. As she stood waiting near an elderly woman and a younger man, the back of her neck prickled. She glanced around, suddenly certain she was being watched. A flash of movement caught her eye, and she turned her head just as a figure disappeared around the corner of a building.

She let out a relieved breath. It was nothing. Just someone hurrying off to an appointment. Her nerves were playing tricks on her, the result of feeling overwhelmed. Who would be watching a stranger in a big city like Milan? Only her imagination, and, as her mother always told her, she had a great one.

CHAPTER 6
SURPRISE OFFER

Stepping off the bus, Elena faced the town centre of Milan. Her eyes shot wide open as she gripped her leather clutch and made her way into the crowds. The smells of fresh coffee beans permeated the air, and the sounds of mopeds and car engines roared past her. Elena craned her neck to see the tall buildings, fascinated by the array of shops, mainly fashion stores, but also bookstores, cafes, and restaurants. It was adrenaline-pumping, and nothing like she'd ever seen before. There was nothing like this in her quiet little village.

Elena walked along Corso di Porta Ticinese and browsed the windows of vintage clothing shops, street wear, and original accessories. Another window display showcased a decorative tiered cake, smaller cupcakes and pastries, which tempted her to taste one of the Italian sweets. She entered the pastry shop and bought a creamy custard cake. Then she went back outside and bit into the softness. Custard dripped over her lips. Wiping it away, she strolled past another store that housed homemade bracelets, watches, and earrings, then a boutique for women displaying chic style dresses and niche brands. There were other stores, some for music lovers that sold books and records; the Vans store selling street wear and urban brands, jewellery, and watches; and other vintage clothing stores. Her Christmases had come all at once.

Elena wondered where to start looking for clothing, but she couldn't afford much even with sale prices. After taking a gander at fast-food restaurants and cafes, she spotted a small clothing store a few doors down that looked more street smart and casual, a better fit for her tastes. She thought about swinging open the door when she smelled a musky cologne behind her. As she turned, Elena came face to face with a towering man in a designer t-shirt that showed his tanned arms, and tight-fitting jeans that displayed his muscular curves.

He smiled. The dimples on both cheeks warmed her body. His hand flicked back his long fringe, revealing the most emerald-green eyes she had ever seen. "Scusi. Can I help you?"

Elena was confused. She shrugged, unable to find her voice.

"I work here," he said, "but you look undecided about whether you wish to go inside or not."

She cleared her throat and came to her senses. The scar on his right eyelid obviously had a story, but suited him. The autumn breeze feathered her cheeks. "Of course." She swung open the door and he followed closely behind, his breath tingling her skin. Goosebumps rose on her neck, and she took in a calming breath. The air was sweet with the scent of cinnamon.

She smiled at a young woman sporting a smart Gucci top, a piercing in her nose, and flower tattoos over both sides of her neck. Elena realised she was staring, then scoured the clothing rack to hide her shame. The shop was big enough to hold a range of trendy clothing, stockings, and accessories, but wouldn't be large enough for much of a crowd during the end-of-season sales. Unfortunately for her, there'd be no end-of-season sales until January. She'd have to wait until then to buy more clothing. For now, she'd have to settle for a few basic needs, just things to get her by as she studied or socialised.

The young man she'd met at the door disappeared into the back of shop and the woman approached her. Elena fumbled through the racks, finding gorgeous autumn ready-to-wear jumpers, fashionable jackets, and knitted mini-skirts.

"Can I help you with anything in particular?" The woman was petite, but her presence was mighty. She exuded a mixture of warmth and power. The mini-skirt she wore displayed long legs underneath tanned fishnet stockings. A purple stripe lined the front part of her scalp while the remainder of her jet-black hair reached down to her waist. It looked glossy and smooth.

Elena turned to her. "Thanks, but I'm just looking for now."

"Sure thing. Just holler when you need help."

Elena nodded, heading back to the rack to find a knitted jumper, black stockings, and a woollen mini-skirt. She held them in her hand when the man she'd met returned. He approached her while the woman at the counter wiped the bench. A few customers entered the store and started browsing.

"So, I've never seen you in our store. Are you a local?"

Elena shook her head. "No, I recently moved to Milan."

He licked his lips and fixed his gaze for a moment. "I'm Francesco, and I actually own this store."

Elena felt his magnetism. "It's a great store. You have beautiful clothes with the latest trends, the finest cuts; exactly what you'd expect from the fashion capital of the world."

Francesco moved closer. "I'll put those in the fitting room for you." Elena continued to browse until he returned a moment later. "So, it sounds like you know a bit about fashion. Why is that?"

Elena felt oddly comfortable talking about herself in his presence.

"I just arrived here from Laurino so I could study fashion design. I'll be starting next month."

"Oh, that's fascinating." He turned to watch the other customers who were chatting with the woman at the counter. Within minutes, the queue had increased with some customers pushing ahead to the front. "Look how busy we've suddenly become. I don't suppose you're looking for a part-time job?" His tone was light, but his expression was serious.

Elena leaned forward, excitement building up inside her. Then the *yes* died in her mouth. What if she wasn't cut out to work in a fancy boutique like this one? Particularly in a large, strange city. How would she cope with the busy pace? In the village, she had never had to manage more than one or two customers at a time, but here in this strange city…it was too hectic. Too overwhelming. "I'm, aah, not sure."

Francesco gave her a reassuring smile. "Anyway, have a think about it while you try on your clothes. I'll speak to you later."

Elena headed into the changing room, tried on her clothes, her chest inflating at the beautiful cut and textures of the fabrics. She was in heaven when she approached the counter and handed out her liras to Francesco.

"So, what do you think? Would you like to work here? We could really use the help, but no pressure." He gave her a brief wink.

It was the wink that did it. How could she let her fears keep her from taking a job that would both solve her financial problems and let her work with the most gorgeous man she'd ever seen? "Okay, I'll give it a go."

He clasped his hands. "Great! When would you like to start?"

Elena shrugged. "Maybe give me a week or so to settle in, but if you need me sooner, I can do that too."

He shook his head. "Not a problem. We'll get you started next week."

"Thank you so much."

"A pleasure. Seeing as you'll be on staff, you're entitled to a discount."

Elena beamed, realising that staying in Milan might not be so bad after all. She had more than one reason to stay now.

CHAPTER 7
A NEW VENTURE

Over the past week, Elena had spoken to her parents and Carla, been reprimanded by Nunziata about leaving a clean glass on the sink, and had cooked meals for her and Emilio. Today, she'd enrolled in her fashion design course. She experienced a flutter of butterflies in her stomach over starting her new job.

Walking along the pavement, she felt a slow drizzle fall over her head and hugged her body for warmth. Her mind drifted back to Francesco, who seemed too good to be true. Was he a ladies' man? She believed that, with his looks, he must be, but that didn't mean she couldn't dream about him, or couldn't have a spring in her step each time his image flashed in her mind. Even getting this job was too good to be true, but that didn't mean she would refuse good things.

Elena was wearing the clothes she'd bought from the store; the woollen mini-skirt, black stockings, the knitted jumper, and a tan scarf she'd brought from home. When the bus pulled over, she stepped onto it, sat in front, and peered through the window. Her heart beat fast as she pondered whether she'd keep up with the frenetic sales pace of a huge city like Milan. The clothing store she'd worked at in Laurino moved at a snail's pace. How could it compare to Milan?

The bus slowed to a stop in the centre of Milan. Elena felt numb all over. Her feet refused to move when she stood up, and the driver ushered her out of the bus. "Hurry up, I don't have all day, lady."

She turned towards the driver, her face flushed. "I'm so sorry." She scurried out and almost slipped off the step as she caught her breath and stood frozen on the cracked footpath. The drizzle had developed into a mild rain, so she took cover under the shop fronts and dodged her way through the crowds. A few men smiled and waved to her. One of them shouted, "Come home with me, carina. I'll give you a good time." She shook her head and didn't respond as she raced her way through.

It took her ten minutes to make her way to the shop. Standing beneath the awning, she wiped away the dampness on her cheeks and shook the water out of her long ponytail.

Then she swung open the door and smiled at the young woman she'd met last week.

"Welcome. Elena, isn't it?" The young woman headed towards Elena in the empty store. "I never got to introduce myself the other day because it was busy, but I'm Loredana." She held out her hand and Elena shook it. Loredana emanated warmth, and Elena instantly felt a connection with the woman.

"Come around the back," Loredana said. "I'll show you how things work with inventory, storage, and the new stock that just came in."

Elena nodded and followed her to the back of the shop. Loredana showed her the staff room, which housed a small television set, a toaster, percolator, and a small fridge. A couple of storage rooms and garbage bins were towards the back of the shop.

The sound of the door alerted them to a customer. They headed to the front, and Loredana prodded Elena towards the customer.

"Can I help you?" Elena asked.

The tall lady smiled and shook her head. "Just browsing for now. Thanks."

Elena went to stand behind the counter, beside Loredana. A few minutes later, Francesco arrived wearing a tight-fitting cotton sweater and dark jeans, a silver chain glinted around his neck. Elena's chest palpitated as he winked at her, joining her behind the counter. "Has Loredana been showing you the ropes?"

"Yes, she's shown me around and explained a bit about the process."

His gaze lingered as he clasped his hands. Then he wandered past her into the back of the store. Her breath returned, and the heat in her body subsided. What was going on with her? So, he was good-looking. Other guys in Laurino were good-looking too. She knew she was fooling herself, though. She'd had a few boyfriends back home without her father knowing, and her body had never responded the way it did now. Francesco was special. He was also way out of her league. Way out of her age-bracket too.

The customer finally approached the counter and laid two hats on it. Elena looked towards Loredana, who nodded. Elena entered the order, took the cash, and packaged the goods. The customer left and Loredana pushed Elena towards the tea room.

21

"Well done! Your first sale. Now go make yourself a coffee. I'll take the next customer."

"Thanks." Elena strolled down towards the room when she was faced with Francesco's back. He was speaking on a telephone that was resting on a small table close to the kitchen bench. His right hand clenched as he shook his head. He suddenly turned around and forced a smile before speaking into the receiver again.

"I have to go." His face reddened. "I said I have to go." He slammed the phone down.

Elena reached for the percolator, then scoured through cupboards for the coffee. She'd just closed her hand around it when she heard Francesco's breath behind her.

"You're making coffee?" he said.

"Would you like one?"

"Sure."

She scooped a teaspoon into the coffee bag and added it into the percolator after adding the water. Turning to him, she watched his gaze fall to the floor and his hands draw through his hair. He looked stressed out, and she wondered exactly what she'd walked in on. Who was he speaking to on the phone? Maybe he had a girlfriend, or maybe he was in some kind of trouble.

Realising it was none of her business, Elena set the coffee on the stove. She would never have the chance to get involved in Francesco's business anyway, so why worry herself?

CHAPTER 8
THE FIRST DAY

Elena walked through the glass doors of the fashion institute after wiping her shoes across the mat. It was October and two weeks had already gone by for her first day of learning. The tiled flooring of Istituto Marangoni was immaculate and the structure very linear and solid as she observed the walkway. Gigantic displays of models dressed in luxurious clothing lined the walls with an array of light fixtures hanging down from the ceiling.

Elena approached reception and was welcomed with a genuine grin. The woman had dimples on her face, which was covered in freckles. She had dark eyes and her hair was tied in a bun.

"May I help you?"

Elena pointed to her letter. "Yes, I need to find this room for my fashion design course."

The woman rose. "Come with me."

Elena followed her guide to a room with a long rectangular table complete with stationery and sketch pads, an array of sewing accessories, a pile of fashion design text books, and a range of fabrics and portfolio books sitting on the table. Mannequins surrounded the back corners of the room. A few other students sat huddled around the table, waiting for the class to commence.

"Well, this is it."

Elena nodded. "Thank you."

"Welcome." The lady left with a sweet smile.

Not wanting to be noticed, Elena snuck inside. The room was eerily quiet, so a few heads turned. Other students scribbled into a notepad or read a book. Elena found a spare seat, hedged in between a young male and a female. She smiled at the woman, whose face flushed, then peered at the man who held out his hand.

"Hi, I'm Angelo. And you are?"

She shook it, but it felt cold and limp. "I'm Elena."

His gaze was intense, so she turned away and set her notebook and pen in front of her. Clasping her hands, she took a deep breath and eyed the groups of students, some of whom looked exotic and appeared to be from different countries, rather than locals. Their attire looked foreign and some of them were speaking what sounded like English while others spoke in French.

Within minutes, a tall professional-looking woman strutted into the room, her high heels resounding against the floor. She looked elegant and solid in build, and her hair was held up in a tight bun. The expression on her face was neutral as she placed her bag and piles of documents at the head of the table.

She took a seat and watched the students. "Welcome to your first year in fashion design. My name is Valentina and I will be your teacher and guide." She cleared her throat, then proceeded to explain housekeeping and details about the course. "In the first year, we'll be looking at the theory of design and carrying out some practical work, involving the architecture of design. We'll also learn about a range of fabrics, creating a portfolio, and the history and art of clothing. In the second year, you'll be focusing on your own personal style and branding, a range of contemporary perspectives, and how art and fashion connect. Finally, in the third year, you'll be looking at creating a collection and all the preparation and research that goes into that, as well as the theory aspect. You'll be preparing an industry portfolio to help you with your future fashion career. Throughout all the years, we'll be discussing and researching all types of fashion such as haute couture, ready-to-wear clothing, and mass market sales. Any questions?"

Elena listened as students put up their hands. Her mind took her elsewhere; to the man beside her. A sense of unease settled in her body as she felt Angelo's eyes on her. At intermittent times, he'd stare and shift himself closer. The potency of his body odour made her want to vomit, but she distracted herself by thinking about Francesco until the woman next to her handed her a fashion design text book.

Valentina continued. "You'll be working from this book to get a handle on the theory of fashion and art, so think of it as your bible."

The woman beside her sighed and turned to Elena. "Excuse me but—aah, would you have a spare pen? Mine's just run out. Sorry."

Elena smiled. "Sure." She picked up her bag from the floor and dived into it to retrieve a pen. Handing it to her classmate, she said, "I'm Elena."

"Isabella. Thank you for the pen." She looked away.

Elena sure had a bunch of interesting people around her. Angelo was a little creepy and Isabella was extremely shy and withdrawn.

At the end of the lesson, as Elena leaned down to grab her bag, Angelo touched her on the shoulder. His fingers lingered and sent an unpleasant tension thrumming through her.

"How about you and me have a bite to eat tonight? What do you say?" He pressed his lips together. Somehow, Elena managed not to cringe.

"Sorry, I can't tonight." She clutched her bag and stationery, then scurried out of the room. What in hell had she got herself into? Tomorrow she'd make sure that this creep didn't sit next to her. Surely, he'd get the hint and leave her alone.

CHAPTER 9
A RUSH OF GUILT

Elena arrived home from class, breathing a sigh of relief at surviving her first day. It had been productive and, aside from a few unpleasant moments with Angelo, she'd loved it. The creative arts had always been her passion, and even though fashion design was her focus, she enjoyed exploring other creative mediums as well. One day, when she built her career in fashion, she'd get a start on writing either a short story or a novel. Or maybe a memoir about her adventures. When she was a famous designer, there was bound to be a market for that.

She found Nunziata in the kitchen embroidering some kind of tablecloth or runner. Nunziata looked up with a curt nod then resumed her stitching. Emilio entered the kitchen, tapping Elena on the shoulder.

He stood beside her as Elena grabbed a glass of water and drank it down. "So how was your first day at Istituto Marangoni?"

"It was amazing." The light she felt in her body spiked her adrenaline. "We get to work from this great design book and we're going to do so much practical stuff. I can't wait."

Nunziata looked up. "Do not forget your chores. I will not have disobedience in this house, do you understand?"

Elena smirked at her brother. "Of course not."

Nunziata glared at Emilio. "And I expect you to at least wash your dishes when you have a snack, or I'll give you something you really won't want to do."

He nodded. "I'm sorry, but I'll be leaving soon so you won't need to worry."

She grunted in response and resumed with her embroidery work.

Elena and Emilio ambled out of the kitchen and into their room. They sat on their respective beds. Emilio clasped and unclasped his hands.

After a moment, he said, "I spoke to Mama on the phone, and she was upset."

Elena leaned forward, wondering if it was her fault. Maybe she regretted letting her come to Milan. Maybe her father was giving her a hard time. "Why?"

"Well, she's become close to Giovanna's daughter, Daniela. They speak about things. About Gregorio and his brother, Aldo."

Elena's throat felt dry. She didn't know whether she could ever forgive Gregorio for what he'd put poor Valeria through. "What about Gregorio? Has he come back?"

"From what I can tell, Gregorio's doing okay in the city but Aldo's apparently in debt. He's been hassling Daniela for money, but she won't give him any. She told Mama that he can't manage his money and wastes it on things like alcohol and parties."

"Does he work?"

"I think so. Some kind of work as a handyman or carpenter, I think, but the money he does make gets wasted."

Elena thought about the money she was spending on her fashion design course. She guessed it had been silly to think there was a chance Giovanna's children didn't know about their mother's bequest to Elena and her siblings. "I guess if we didn't get a share of Giovanna's money, he'd have more of it."

Emilio clenched his hands and shook his head. "Don't you get guilty on me. This Aldo guy would've squandered more of her money, so it's his own fault. Giovanna was insistent on us getting a share of it."

"You don't think her kids hate her for that? I mean, that they got less of a share?"

Emilio shrugged. "Definitely not Daniela. She's generous and warm, but as for Gregorio and Aldo, it's hard to know. I mean, who cares anyway? Giovanna put that request in her will, and unless they want to contest it, we get to keep part of her inheritance."

Elena smiled. "When did you get so wise?"

"Someone must've taught me. Maybe you."

"So why is Mama upset?"

Emilio hesitated. "I think she's just sad for Giovanna. That she had two sons who've given her hell. She worries about Daniela having to deal with Aldo too."

Elena nodded. "Mama worries too much." She moved towards his bed and wrapped her brother in her arms. "I love you, Emilio. I don't ever want to be fighting like Giovanna's children. Life's too short."

"I know, but that will never happen to us. We're too close and we trust each other."

She rose. "Why don't we go and cook dinner and see if Nunziata would like my famous pasta Arrabbiata. She can't say no to that."

He laughed and they walked out of their room. All the while, Elena contemplated how Gregorio and Aldo were a weird pair. She wondered whether Gregorio had changed or whether he was still the same obsessive guy who liked control. She thought of the ways he'd hurt Valeria—stalking her, coming between her and her closest friend, telling Papa tales about her that had led to vicious beatings. He'd even got Valeria's boyfriend killed, though it had been technically an accident.

Elena swallowed hard. Gregorio had to have changed. Everyone said so. Surely, he wouldn't make trouble for them now.

CHAPTER 10
A NIGHT OUT

A week later, Loredana flicked through a pile of liras and deposited them into the cash register. She smiled at the customer who walked out carrying bags of winter clothing. Then she cleared up the counter by storing the clothes that customers didn't want back on the racks. The door swung open and Elena ambled inside, a weary expression on her face. She was still getting her bearings in this huge city. The poor girl!

Loredana smiled. "Hi, Elena. Are you enjoying the work so far?"

Elena watched her put the remainder of the clothes back in place. "Great. I'm loving it. Thanks again for the opportunity."

"Oh, that was Francesco's doing, not mine," Loredana said.

Francesco waltzed in from the back, his shoulders straightening as he approached the counter. His eyes lit up at the sight of Elena. The guy had it bad. "Did someone mention my name?"

Elena blushed. "I'm just glad to be given this opportunity. Thanks, Francesco."

"No worries." He lingered in his gaze and his hand squeezed her shoulder. "Anyway, I only came by to grab something, and then I'll be leaving. Have a good night." He let go of Elena's shoulder and she fixed her gaze as he rushed out the door.

Loredana smiled to herself and turned to Elena. "I see the way he looks at you."

Elena stared. "Who?"

"Francesco of course." She chuckled. "I can tell he likes you."

Elena blushed again. "He doesn't like me. He's simply being friendly."

"Hmmm. Anyway, how about we have a night out? There's this disco you'll absolutely love. The owners are thinking about having some of my paintings on their wall."

Elena's eyes widened. "You're an artist?"

She nodded. "Just an amateur at the moment, but I do the odd art class and occasionally sell some of my paintings. They're mainly abstract, but I do landscapes as well. Have you heard of Salvador Dali?"

"Of course."

"Well, he inspires me in my abstracts. I love his use of the concept of time, too."

"I'd love to see your work. I mean, maybe one day we can join forces—your artistry and my fashion design."

Loredana nodded. "Anyway, are we on for tonight?"

Elena's cheeks tinged with excitement. "Okay."

Loredana hoped she and Elena could be friends. She felt an instant connection with her new co-worker and was glad to see the spark that seemed to be growing between her and Francesco. She wondered if Francesco would realise how kind-hearted Elena was. His previous girlfriends seemed to be shallow and without substance. Elena definitely had substance.

***

Elena strolled towards Loredana, who wore knee-high boots over tight jeans, a tight-fitting blouse that showed her cleavage, and a heavy winter jacket.

They were standing in front of a boutique. Elena looked around. "So, where's the disco?"

Loredana beamed. "You're standing right in front of it. It's a disco *through* a

boutique. The designer purposely made it that way."

Elena cocked her head and took in the window display, the quirky wooden sign, the frosted glass door with the bell above it. You would never guess it was the entrance to a disco.

Prodding Elena through the door, Loredana said, "Let's go in."

The loud sounds of Pooh's "Pensiero" came up on the speakers as Elena pushed through the crowds behind Loredana. Smoke and dust filled the air, and young men ogled the two women. Elena ignored them, but Loredana flirted with a few passers-by. What was she getting herself into? She'd never been to a disco. The noise was deafening, and she couldn't hear her friend's voice among the sounds. Loredana mouthed something to Elena.

"What?"

Loredana moved over to an empty table and stood beside it. "You stay here, and I'll get us some drinks. An aperitivo and some nibbly snacks?"

Elena shrugged. "I've never tried it but sure, surprise me."

Elena waited with her hands clasped, her eyes turning away from a bearded man who gawked at her. He swaggered his way forward. "Ciao, bella! How about a dance?"

Elena shook her head. "No thanks. I'm waiting for my friend."

He walked away, but moments later, another man with hair that covered most of his eyes approached. "Can I get you a drink?"

"My friend's getting me a drink, but thanks anyway."

He licked his lips and got close. "You have beautiful eyes, carina. And your hair is absolutely divine. How about we dance?"

"No thanks. I'm good." *Where was Loredana?*

Elena turned away to give him the hint. Eventually he stormed off. When Loredana returned with two tall glasses, Elena breathed in relief. "Thank God you're back. These men here won't leave me alone."

Loredana threw her head back in a chuckle. "That's what these Italian nightclubs are like. Men so desperate, but I can tell you that probably ninety per cent of these men are married."

Elena changed the subject, sipping her strong aperitif. "I'm curious about Francesco's scar. Do you know how he got it?"

Loredana shook her head. "Not a clue. When I did ask him once, he said he'd had some kind of accident, but didn't elaborate." She pondered. "I got the feeling there was more to it."

"Like what?"

She shrugged. "I don't know." Loredana fixed her gaze on Elena. "Anyway, tell me about yourself."

Elena talked about her family, her work in the store and on the farm, and mentioned the few relationships she'd had. She found Loredana easy to talk to.

"Some friends of mine are going to this other disco next week. Care to join us?"

"Sure. I don't really know anyone here, so why not?"

Loredana grabbed her hand. "Well, you do now, and you'll love my friends."

Their friendship moment was disrupted when a familiar face headed towards her.

It was Angelo. "Elena, what a surprise."

She drew back. *Oh, no!*

He gestured to the man beside him. "This is my friend, Marco. This is Elena. And you are?" He turned to Loredana.

She shook Angelo's hand. "I'm Loredana."

Unfortunately for Elena, Loredana was admiring his friend, who had brown wavy hair and a rugged body. He was handsome, but she couldn't say the same for Angelo who might've been better-looking if he took care of his grooming. Maybe there was something deeper beneath his abrasive surface.

"Would you like to dance?" Marco asked Loredana.

She turned to Elena. "Is that okay with you, Elena?"

Elena wanted to say no, but she wouldn't stop her friend's fun. "Of course. Go ahead."

After they rushed off, Elena felt Angelo's leg rub against hers as he moved his chair closer to her. "I'm glad we're finally alone."

Elena shifted her chair back, a chill racking her body.

After small talk and the end of her drink, Elena spotted Loredana kissing Marco. His hands were pawing at her breasts and bottom as he pressed her up against a wall. Elena cringed. They might as well get a room, the way they were carrying on.

"Looks like someone other than us is having their own fun." Angelo watched his friend and Loredana for a moment, then turned to Elena with hunger in his eyes. "How about you and me have our own little fun?"

Elena's breathing shallowed. "I don't think so."

His eyes darkened, but he remained silent.

This was going to be a long night.

CHAPTER 11
A STRANGE LIAISON

Elena drew back at Valentina's next assignment.

"Any issues, Elena?" Valentina asked, tilting her head.

Elena shook her head. "No. All good."

"Well then, I suggest you and Angelo look at the third chapter of the book to arrange your project. Time is pressing on."

Nausea roiled through Elena's stomach. What had she done to deserve working with Angelo on this project? Did he put the teacher up to this? Was he punishing her for the other night? She cast her mind back to the disco, remembering how Angelo had flirted and made his move. She'd rejected him, and ultimately, he gave her the silent treatment until his friend Marco had returned with Loredana.

The four of them soon left and shared a taxi but Loredana stayed at Marco's house for the night while Angelo silently went on his way. Elena couldn't believe how childish Angelo had been. If she wasn't interested, he had to accept that.

Angelo pursed his lips and flicked through the text book. He skimmed the section on haute couture and prêt-à-porter fashion styles, then threw the book towards her. It landed with a thud on the table and the page was lost. She turned to him, but he focused away from her to jot down his own notes. He shifted his chair further away as if she was poisonous.

Elena sighed and made her own notes after finding the page. She shifted her eyes to her other side. Isabella's face reddened as she squirmed under the dominance of a fellow student who towered over her and controlled rather than shared the book. Isabella sighed but managed to soldier on by taking her own notes and biting down on her lower lip. "Are you okay?" Elena asked.

Isabella shrugged, and her face blushed further.

"How about we grab dinner after class?"

Isabella frowned and hesitated. "Sorry, but—I'm busy tonight."

"No worries. Maybe next time." Elena turned back to Angelo, who managed to grab the book off the table and thumb through the pages with a bored expression on his face.

"Well, are we working together or not?" said Angelo. "I seem to be doing all the work around here. Some of us don't have the time to socialise."

Elena cleared her throat and shifted.

Throughout the rest of the assignment, Angelo sent her dirty stares and monopolised the text book. Once Valentina got their attention, she turned to the class and asked for feedback on their project.

When all the groups had shared, Valentina gave a lecture about the architecture of design, then started setting up a video. Angelo flicked Elena's pen off the table with his elbow. She huddled to the floor and reached out for her pen but couldn't see it anywhere.

Angelo said, "I'll get your pen for you." As he joined her on the floor, she spotted the pen out of her reach. Angelo extended his arm, but rather than reach for the pen, he reached out to squeeze her right breast.

Wincing, Elena shoved his hand away and scrambled to her feet. Who cared about her damn pen anyway? She suddenly felt violated and wanted to tell the others what he'd done, but she felt ashamed and embarrassed.

Elena clasped her hands and Angelo handed back her pen. He smirked as if he'd won a competition. She wanted to slap him. Embarrassed or not, if this harassment continued, she'd have to speak to Valentina about his wretched behaviour.

Her face warmed as she moved her chair around to face the screen, keeping plenty of room between her seat and Angelo's. As Valentina started the video about beginning a career in design and artistry, Elena sensed Angelo's eyes boring into her back. A low voice startled her.

"You're not so in control now, are you, Elena?"

She swallowed, refusing to be controlled the way her father had controlled her. Turning around, she looked Angelo square in the eye, and whispered, "No one likes a sore loser who can't accept rejection."

His eyes narrowed, and he pulled back like a child. Elena looked away and breathed a sigh of relief. Hopefully now he would treat her with respect. She refused to be bullied by anyone, but as she watched him sulk, his expression slowly darkened into something deeper. Something more dangerous. It made her feel uneasy.

CHAPTER 12
HARASSMENT

The driver beeped for Emilio to get into the waiting taxi. Elena wrapped her arms around him and wiped her tears away with a shaky hand. She snuggled into his warmth. They pulled apart, and Emilio turned away as if ashamed of his own tears.

"You take care of yourself. At least write me a letter on the odd occasion."

Elena sniffled. "I will, and please call me as soon as you get home. I want to make sure you get there safe."

He nodded. "I'll let Mama know that you've made some nice friends here and that you're safe where you're staying." He chuckled. "Nunziata might not be the friendliest person on this earth but at least she's giving you a roof over your head."

Elena chuckled. "True."

Elena watched as he handed his suitcase to the driver, who shoved it into the boot. Then Emilio rushed into the taxi, waving as it pulled away. Elena's shoulders slumped. She would miss Emilio. Her safety net was gone but she knew how to take care of herself. Her father never liked her independent streak, but he'd learned to respect her after all these years. Valeria had paved the way for her, having borne the brunt of his cruelty. He would never have got away with that cruelty with Elena. She would've made sure of it.

Elena made her way into the house and spotted Nunziata setting down the phone, but not on its cradle.

She turned towards Elena. "There is a phone call for you. He wouldn't give me his name."

Elena headed to the phone and picked it up. "Hello." Silence. "Hello, is anyone there? It's Elena here." More silence, but she heard raspy breathing. "Hello. Is anyone there?" She waited. Nothing came but a resounding click.

Elena found Nunziata in the kitchen. "What did the person on the phone sound like?"

She shrugged. "How should I know?"

Elena breathed out. "Did he sound young, old or have an accent?"

Nunziata turned back to her embroidery. "Young, I guess." She looked Elena square in the eye. "I won't have you gallivanting around with some hoodlum. Whoever that was, I don't need any trouble."

"But that's the thing. Whoever was on the phone just hung up on me. I don't know who it was." She shifted her posture. "And I am not the type to make trouble."

Nunziata rose from the table, approached Elena, and grabbed her hard by the shoulders. "Just the way you answered me suggests trouble." She sighed heavily. "If you're going to give me issues, I want you out of here." She glared. "I don't need this in my life."

Elena took calming breaths. She pulled away from Nunziata's stubby hands. "I am not in any trouble, Nunziata." She turned on her heel. "I'm sorry I asked."

Nunziata pursed her lips. "And what the hell is that supposed to mean? I won't take mocking from you either. How dare you answer me back? You've been warned."

Elena tried a soft approach. "What is going on here? You seem rattled and I'd like to know why."

Nunziata turned away. She fixed her gaze on Elena as if pondering whether to say anything. Instead she stormed off.

Elena shook her head and walked to her bedroom. She lay back on the bed wondering what was wrong with that woman. Something was definitely going on with her because anyone normal wouldn't react that strongly to her question about the caller. Something had happened to her. It wasn't fair, though, that not only did she have to deal with Nunziata, she had Angelo too.

Elena closed her eyes and relished the quiet for a few moments. Then she sank into the bed and felt herself falling deeper and deeper into slumber. A noise outside her window jolted her awake. She got up, opened her window, and peered out. There was nothing unusual outside. The wind. A few trees. Shadows in the gaps between the hedges and the house. A few people walking down the block. A flock of birds soaring, but nothing much else. She returned to her bed and gave it no more thought. Probably just a cat.

She wriggled under the covers and dreamed of being chased by someone without a face. She ran until her legs gave out and the person behind snatched her. She was sinking into a dark abyss, when she woke up. Her face was damp with sweat and her legs shook as she tiptoed to the bathroom and washed her face. Staring back at her from the mirror were dark circles under her eyes that made her look older than her twenty years. An uneasy feeling showed in her eyes. Maybe she was already missing Emilio.

Returning to her bedroom, Elena noticed a folded piece of paper stuck underneath her window. Had she forgotten to lock her window?

Unfolding the note, it read:

"Do not EVER think you are safe. You are NOT safe!!"

Elena dropped the note as if it burned to the touch. She put her hand on her heart and felt the racing beats while chills tingled up and down her spine. She looked around as if someone was about to jump on her, then hugged herself and closed her eyes for a moment to instil a relaxed state. She approached the window and locked it. Why would someone invade her safe space? She wondered if it was a man from the disco, but what if it wasn't? What if it was Angelo? He certainly seemed the type to do such a thing. The more she thought about it, the more certain she was. It had to be him.

CHAPTER 13
A NEW FRIEND

Valentina clapped her hands. "Attention everyone. Attention." Isabella turned to a blank page in her notebook, eager for the day's lesson. Valentina waited for the students to quieten down, then continued. "Today we'll be exploring an array of fabrics and the types of fabrics that go with particular designs. We've got a range of fabrics on that table in the back." She pointed. "And we'll discuss all of them while you get a feel for the material. The theme here is to get an idea of the types of fabrics that match certain kinds of designs. You'll be learning about synthetics, cottons, woollens, acrylics, and the list goes on."

Her gaze swept the room. "Now you have to start to think about designing clothes that are not only aesthetically pleasing but also functional. In other words, designing clothes that can be worn in particular situations such as work, leisure, or evening wear." She paced the room and looked at each student square in the eye. "You might get an interest in designing for the mass market or you might want to design haute couture for the individual. We also have to keep in mind the ongoing trends. But not only that, you can also design original work, and that might be your speciality in the future."

Isabella closed her notebook. Apparently, this would be a hands-on assignment, so she wouldn't need to take notes. Maybe she and Elena could work together; they shared a similar enthusiasm for the class. While Valentina explained the assignment, Isabella glanced towards Elena, but the other girl didn't catch her gaze. Instead, she sat with her back stiff and her head down, shifting in her seat until her upper body was at an uncomfortable-looking angle.

It didn't take long for Isabella to understand why. A few aisles away, Angelo was staring at Elena in a creepy way. Isabella had felt relieved when Angelo had sat next to another fellow student rather than near her and Elena, but that didn't stop him from looking at Elena intermittently. Apparently, Angelo was making the most of staring at Elena from a distance.

Elena shot a quick glance in Angelo's direction. He winked at her. What a jerk. His expression was dark, and Elena jerked her gaze away.

As Valentina waved them towards the back of the room, Isabella stood up and moved closer to Elena, who followed behind her towards the fabric table. All the students ran their hands through the fabrics while Valentina gave a spiel about each material. "I'd like you to cut out all these fabrics and stick your small samples into your sketch book. That way, when you create your own collection, you'll get ideas of which types of fabrics to use."

Isabella started cutting out fabric while others did the same. Elena turned to her unexpectedly. "So, how are you enjoying the course so far?"

Isabella stopped cutting and looked up. "It's great. I'm loving it. And you?"

"I'm glad I'm here. I made the right decision I think."

Isabella started to answer, then lost her train of thought when Angelo edged close to Elena, holding the scissors dangerously close to her waist. Elena shifted to Isabella's other side.

Isabella nodded her approval. *Great idea.* "Are you okay?" she asked.

Elena nodded. Angelo glared, then resumed his cutting. He was taunting Elena, and Isabella wished there was something she could do. The poor girl was obviously resilient but having a creep like Angelo taunt you was too much for anyone.

They resumed theory work back at their table, and Angelo's eyes fixated on Elena as if searching her soul. When Elena ignored him and bowed her head to take notes, Isabella touched her shoulder, sympathising with her. Angelo was definitely a creep.

At the end of class, Isabella found herself walking beside Elena as they exited the building. Huddles of students rushed behind her while others rushed ahead of her. The sounds of engines and street smells permeated the air as she immersed herself in the crisp wind. A hard shove from behind propelled her forward. Then Elena crashed into her, and Isabella stumbled over the kerb and into the road. A sharp pain shot through her ankle, and she landed hard on her side.

"Ouch, my ankle." Isabella pushed herself into a sitting position and rubbed her ankle. It throbbed and tingled. She hoped it wasn't broken.

Elena bobbed down. "I'm sorry! It's not broken, is it?"

"I don't think so. Probably no more than a strain."

Elena pulled her up from the road as onlookers asked if she needed help. "Can you walk on it?"

Isabella nodded. "I can, but it hurts."

Elena held her around the waist. "We'll get you to a doctor."

Isabella shook her head. "No need. I just need to rest it. It's starting to settle, so I should be fine by tomorrow."

"Why don't we sit in one of those shops for a while so you can rest it before going home?"

She nodded. "Okay."

Isabella hobbled while Elena held her arm around Isabella's waist. They entered a coffee shop along the shopping strip a short walk away, settling on a table near the window.

A short, stocky waiter came to take their order. They ordered cafe lattes.

Elena pulled up her shoulders and shivered. "What happened back there?"

Isabella leaned forward. "I don't know. Did someone push you?"

Elena nodded. "I felt a shove from behind."

"Did you see who it was?"

Elena hesitated. "No, I didn't."

Isabella barely knew Elena, but there was obvious tension between her and Angelo. *Would it be wise to mention it?*

Isabella knit her brows and took the plunge. "Is something going on between you and Angelo? He keeps staring at you in class. It's a little weird."

Elena took time replying. "He made a move and I rejected him." Isabella listened as Elena added more detail about how she attended a disco and how she'd rebuffed Angelo's advances.

The waiter brought their orders.

Isabella added sugar and stirred. "So, what are you going to do about him?"

Elena sipped her latte. "I don't know. Ignore him for now, but if he doesn't stop hassling me I'll speak to Valentina."

"I doubt she'll be able to do anything. He's a student and so far, hasn't done anything wrong, other than stare at you in class."

Elena opened her mouth as if to say something else, but she closed it again. Had something else happened with Angelo? Something worse?

"So where are you from?" Elena asked.

Isabella angled her head. "I'm from Salerno. And you?"

"I'm from Laurino. I've never been out of the village until now. It's exciting."

They exchanged talk about their families and fashion design dreams. Isabella recounted how her father had recently died, and how much she missed him.

Luckily for her she had a new friend. After worrying about coming to a huge city, she needed all the friends she could get.

CHAPTER 14
A TAD CLOSER

Leaning against the counter of the store, Elena smiled to herself. She'd made a new friend in Isabella and found they had a lot in common.

The sound of the door opening rattled in her ears, and her heart flipped as Francesco walked through it. What was he doing here? She'd expected Loredana to be working today. He grinned. "Hi, Elena. Loredana's not feeling well so I'm taking over today."

"Oh—okay. No worries." She felt her face redden and her hands grew clammy. Francesco neared her with a sweet smile. His eyes glued to hers, he reached out and gently brushed a strand of hair away from her eye. Then he dropped his hand and rushed to the back like a thunderstorm.

What had just happened?

A touch of disappointment filled her when she barely registered the voice of a customer entering the store. She turned to the chubby woman wearing loads of bling around her wrists and neck.

"Can you help me, please? I need a whole new wardrobe for winter, and pronto. I don't have a lot of time."

"Of course," Elena said. "What are you looking for in particular?"

She waited for a response, but the woman headed to the knitwear racks without answering. Then Elena felt Francesco's presence behind her. The strong musky scent of his cologne overwhelmed her.

He cleared his throat, and she turned to face him and walked back towards the counter.

He leaned in. "That lady's a nightmare. If you like, I can deal with her."

Elena shook her head. "No, let me."

Francesco shrugged. "It's your funeral."

Elena eyed the woman scouring the attire. With a rough hand, she messed up the straightness of the clothes, leaving some hanging above the rack and others hanging below. Clothes fell to the floor, but she didn't pick them up. Eventually she selected an assortment of accessories, pants, jumpers, and skirts, then threw

43

them on the counter. "Ring that up for me, and hurry up about it. I have an urgent appointment."

Elena put on her widest smile. Internally, she wanted to slap the woman. "Are you sure you don't want to try them on first?"

"If I wanted to try them on, I would have. Besides, they are exactly my size." She pursed her lips. "Now get on with it."

"Of course," Elena said, her stomach tightening.

Her hands quivered as Francesco eyed her, his body in close proximity. He whispered, "Just breathe." He packed the bags for her while she rang up the order.

Elena handed the bags to the lady, who stormed out with a grunt.

"That lady will return for exchanges. It's a habit of hers," Francesco said. "What does she expect when she doesn't even try them on? You handled her very well. I'm impressed."

She blushed again. "Thanks."

A few customers later, Francesco suggested they have a morning coffee break. Stepping into the staff room, he picked out the percolator from the cupboard and prepared two steaming cups of espresso. He handed one to Elena and sat opposite her at the table. His eyes lingered, and Elena broke the tension.

"So, have you always wanted to own your own boutique?"

"Pretty much. I love working my own hours, love fashion, and love this city."

"And have you always lived in Milan?"

Francesco hesitated. "No."

She sipped her coffee, intrigued. "Where were you from originally?"

He paled and looked past her. "Not too far from here. Would you like another coffee? I know I need one." He rose and filled his own cup.

"No, I'm fine, thanks."

He sat back down. "Why don't you tell me about your life? Your family?"

Elena disclosed details of her family, her friends, and about Valeria's move to Australia. She contained the butterflies in her stomach, not wanting to appear dazzled by his fixed gaze

He listened in closely. "You know, you are so easy to talk to. You're an amazing woman, Elena." He seemed about to reach out for her hand but moved his back, his brows lifting. I'll go out front. You can take a few more minutes."

What just happened? What was he so afraid of? Did he have feelings for her or was he merely being polite? Maybe he had a girlfriend.

She heard a noise out front; voices interacting. Elena got up and headed to the front of the store. A delivery man exited the shop.

"Chrysanthemums. Why were these flowers delivered here?" Elena asked.

Francesco turned to her. "These were sent to you, but there's no name."

She noticed the pink tinge, a chill running down her spine.

Francesco's eyes darkened. "Why would someone send you flowers of death? These flowers are for funerals."

Elena shrugged. "I wish I knew." The shop seemed to be closing in on her as she wondered who would do such a horrible thing.

CHAPTER 15
AN EXPLORATION

Elena stared at the flowers, totally oblivious to Francesco standing beside her.

His hand squeezed her shoulder. "Are you okay?"

Elena nodded. "I'm fine," she lied. Turning away, she picked up the discarded clothing on the counter and floor. She had to keep busy and not think of those dark flowers.

"So you have no idea who could've sent you these?"

She shook her head. "Probably whoever sent them didn't know the meaning of the flowers."

"You're probably right." Francesco approached, his fingers reaching for her chin, and tilting her face towards him. He leaned forward, and Elena's breath stopped. Her surroundings evaporated as she lingered on his eager, hungry eyes and parting lips. Was he about to kiss her?

The moment was lost when the phone rang in the staff room. Francesco whispered something under his breath. He stepped out back with a slouched posture.

Elena's fingers tingled as she thought about his proximity. She walked over to the staff room, curious about the call. It had to be for Francesco as no one she knew had her work number.

She strained without success to hear, so she crept closer. Peeking in, she observed his eye twitching and the firm grip of the phone as his face flushed. He whispered into the phone, looking anything but relaxed. That was the second time she'd seen him agitated over a phone call. Who was he speaking to? Did she have a right to ask? Not at all.

Her guilt got the better of her, so she scurried back to the counter and tidied around the clothing racks. Francesco soon returned and forced a smile at her.

At closing time, Francesco said, "I'll put up the closed sign and you can balance the till. Then we'll head home."

Elena nodded and got to work, all the while sensing that Francesco was miles away. She thought about tonight's evening out at the disco with Loredana and Isabella. She was looking forward to it. She wondered if Francesco might be there, but she doubted it. Surely, he would've mentioned it.

He stood awkwardly beside her, staring at the ground. She kept her gaze on her task, imagining she could hear his heartbeat and feel the warmth of his body. When she finished counting the takings, she picked up her bag and walked out of the store with Francesco.

He grabbed her by the hand. "Why don't I drive you home? My car's not too far from here."

Elena was tongue-tied. "No, that's okay. I don't mind taking the bus."

Francesco pulled her in the other direction, his arms warming her skin and creating goosebumps. "Come on, I don't mind. Why catch the bus when I have my car here?"

Elena succumbed to his charm and they walked alongside each other, barely mindful of the crowds and the shopping strip of designer wear. She watched the way his taut muscles stood out under the folds of his shirt and how he often flicked his smooth hair out of his eyes. The scar on the upper part of his right eyelid looked even more endearing than before. She wondered again how he'd got it.

He owned a white Fiat and had parked in an outdoor parking area. Once they were ready to exit the crowded area, Elena avoided Francesco's intense, soulful stares. She gave him her address.

He nodded. "I know exactly where that is."

Elena peered through the windows, grateful for the lift. He drove at an average speed in spite of beeping drivers wanting to pass him and slow drivers holding them up.

After engaging in several minutes of small talk, Francesco said, "So . . . you must have an admirer, Elena."

Was he happy about that? She couldn't tell.

"It's just somebody's idea of a joke," she said.

He took his eyes away from the road for a moment. "Who do you know that's male? Someone at school?"

Elena shrugged, not wanting to disclose how someone was harassing her. She shifted the conversation. "So, are you close to your family?"

Francesco turned back to the road and nodded. "Mostly, they're great."

"And where did you say you came from?" Silence. "Francesco, where are you from?"

"Aah—a small village in Salerno."

What was he hiding? "Where exactly?"

Francesco suddenly beeped the car in front of them. "Don't you just hate slow drivers?"

"I've never driven, so can't say I do."

He frowned. "Are you planning to learn?"

"Eventually, but right now I want to focus on my studies. There's plenty of time to drive."

He nodded, then looked back at the road. As he neared her residence, he stopped by the kerb. "I guess I'll see you soon, Elena. Thanks for all your hard work today."

Elena fumbled with her seatbelt, pressing the button that wouldn't unfasten. "Damn! It's stuck."

Francesco unbuckled his belt and leaned in, pressing the button several times until it finally unbuckled. Instead of moving back to his position, he lifted his hand and stroked her cheek. "God, you're beautiful." His lips parted. Elena's gaze fell on his lips, and her body trembled with excitement. His lips inched closer to hers. The desire in his eyes was obvious. As if he wanted so badly to kiss her. Her heart stirred. Her hands tingled. Her mind felt fuzzy. This was it. He was getting closer and closer.

The moment was lost again when he kissed her briefly on the cheek, cleared his throat, turned away and re-buckled himself. "I'll see you, Elena. You'd better go."

Her shoulders deflated. "See you." Her fingers slipped off the house key when she reached for it. She picked up the key, swung open the car door, and rushed out. A huge gap filled her chest, and confusion and disappointment flooded her mind. He'd seemed so close to making a move. She'd been so hopeful and giddy at the idea of the almost-kiss, she couldn't believe it hadn't happened. As she'd told herself before, he must have a girlfriend or maybe he was married. She knew she was reading the signs that he liked her, so there had to be some reason for his sudden attack of cold feet. Elena didn't turn back, but she didn't hear the car driving off until after she'd stepped inside.

CHAPTER 16
A CHANGE OF SCENERY

Francesco watched Elena rush into her house. When she dropped
her key and leaned over to pick it up, his breath caught in his throat
at the sight of her beautiful, flexible body. How could such beauty
exist? How could he be such an idiot? He wasn't sure what he was
doing with her, but he couldn't let it get anywhere. It was a bad
idea. He had way too much baggage. She deserved better.
Francesco put the car in drive and accelerated, still haunted by
Elena's mesmerising eyes. He thought about the disco tonight.
Loredana had invited him but he had declined out of logic. Now he
would accept her invitation out of desire. He wanted to be near
Elena. Nothing more than that. He wanted to relish her company,
her intelligence, her warmth, and her wisdom. Who cared what
anyone else thought? Tonight, he planned to get to know Elena a
lot more, enough—he hoped—to become close friends. That was
all they could ever be.

It was a short drive to his apartment from the place where
Elena was staying. By the time he pulled into his parking slot, the
thought of seeing Elena had made his mouth feel dry and his face
feel hot. He tossed his keys onto a table near the entrance and
entered the open kitchen area to pour himself cold water from the
fridge. He sat on a stool at his oak timber table and sipped on his
drink. He rested his elbows on the table and raked his hand through
his hair. He'd come so close to kissing her. An image of her face
continued to haunt him. It was driving him crazy.

He stepped into the shower to cool off in spite of the near-
winter climate. He'd never felt so intensely about anyone before.
The other women he'd gone out with were either shallow or sweet,
but his heart had never soared the way it did now. He couldn't
believe he'd fallen so hard, so fast. If only it could work out. But it
couldn't. He had to put his feelings aside and think logically about
the situation.

Turning off the faucet, Francesco towelled off and
dressed in a fitted white silk shirt, black pants, and Italian Gucci
shoes. He'd always taken pride in his appearance. He liked nice
clothes and always made sure he had something special to wear.

Besides, a boutique owner should always wear nice clothes so he could be his own brand.

Francesco sprayed on cologne, brushed his hair, and listened to the radio until it was time to leave for the disco. His heart beat fast as he ambled to his car, the cold wind brushing his cheeks, the trees surrounding him swaying in the breeze. Dark clouds shadowed the blue skies, and a trickle of rain fell on his cheek. Smells of car fumes grounded him as he stepped into his car and drove off.

Once he arrived, his hands shook as he made his way to the entrance. Francesco eyed the colourful light-fittings hanging down the ceiling and the storm of bodies pushing against each other. The small stage held microphones and disc jockey equipment with cords hanging down. Multiple steps lined the stage. He walked over lino flooring with bits of discarded rubbish, cigarette butts, and wet patches. No doubt patrons had passed out and spilled their drinks. Chairs surrounded small tables, and he roamed the room for any sight of Elena, Loredana, and her friends.

He headed to the bar and bought himself an iced Scotch. His eyes lingered on a woman leaning towards him, staring him down.

"Buy me a drink?"

Her breasts were at least a double D but in spite of being gorgeous, she had cold, dark eyes. "Sorry, I'm waiting for friends."

Without watching the woman's response, he turned around and spotted Elena watching their exchange. *Was Elena jealous?* The woman stormed off.

Loredana punched him on the shoulder. "Hey, Francesco. We finally made it. The bus was such a drag, but we got here in the end."

Francesco nodded and greeted two of her female friends who were as perky as Loredana. They smiled in response.

Elena headed towards him with another girl who wore a bob-style haircut and dimples. "Hi, Francesco. This is Isabella from the institute."

"Pleased to meet you, Isabella." He shook her hand, which was cold and limp. The poor girl looked shy.

"You too," she whispered.

Francesco looked over Elena, who wore a figure-hugging black dress that revealed her small cleavage, tanned arms, and slim figure. His pulse quickened. This woman was seriously hot. She turned around and the criss-crossed straps across her back revealed the smoothest skin he'd ever seen. For a moment, he could barely speak.

Get a hold of yourself, man.

He tore his gaze away from her and took out his wallet to pay for drinks for everyone. He handed them out individually and found an empty table. He noticed Isabella staring, but he quickly looked away. She was pretty, and seemed sweet, but his heart was with Elena, who seemed to do her best to avoid his eyes. Instead, she engaged in conversation with Isabella and occasionally with Loredana and her friends.

His own friends had said they'd drop by later in the night. He wished they'd hurry. He needed the distraction. He couldn't stop looking at Elena. The way she licked her lips. The way she held her palm against her chest when she laughed, and the way she drew her slim hand through her long hair. Even the way she held a confident posture in spite of her naivety in a big city. She may have come from a small village, but with her spirited personality, she fit very easily into Milan.

After exchanging small talk with Loredana, he froze when a short, chubby man approached Elena and stopped mere inches from her face. She shifted in her seat and moved back but he kept leaning in towards her. Even Isabella looked uneasy with the exchange. *Who the hell was this cocky bastard?*

CHAPTER 17
LIAISON

Loredana smiled at the way Elena politely refused the man's invitation to dance. Even better was the way Francesco clenched his hands but stayed back, watching the exchange. Those two were so cute together. She hoped they'd figure it out soon. As her friends moved over to the dance floor, Loredana walked over to the ladies' room. A large hand suddenly stopped her from entering.

"Hi there. Don't I know you? You're Maria, aren't you?"

Loredana drew back, mesmerised by the man's solid build, dark eyes, crooked nose over a squarish-shaped face, and the fullest lips she had ever seen. She could kiss those lips right now. His cologne was a mixture of citrus and wood. What a cheap line, she thought, but he looked like a god. "No, I'm not Maria." She made her way into the ladies' room.

"I'll be here when you come out."

Loredana frowned as she entered and thought about this mystery man. In spite of the cliché, he had to be too good to be true. Surely he wouldn't wait for her.

After washing her hands and taking her time, she exited the room. Surprisingly he was standing alongside her and shook her hand. "I'm Biagio. Pleased to meet you."

"Loredana." He pushed her towards an empty corner of the disco and looked her up and down. "I need to get back to my friends." She couldn't see them from where she was standing, but her friends had company, so it wasn't like she was leaving them alone. Surely, she could spend time here with Biagio. He might turn out to be her one true love.

"So, tell me about yourself," he said.

Loredana filled him in on her family and work and he then reciprocated.

He watched her intently. "I'm a carpenter by trade, work as a contractor. I'm currently taking a break from the grind of hard work. You know how it is."

She nodded. "Are you from Milan?" Loredana asked.

He shook his head. "No, from a village. I miss coming to the big cities, you know. I love all these little surprises and beautiful women."

Oh, not another womaniser. "So why are you with me when there are so many beautiful women around?"

"You are the most beautiful so far." He leaned in, brushed her cheek with his thumb, and kissed her gently on the lips. "So beautiful!" His lips tantalised her further, then his tongue. His hands wrapped around her waist and squeezed her bottom to press her closer towards him. He gave a little moan, and reluctantly, they pulled apart.

"So, who are you with here tonight?" he asked, his voice husky with desire.

Loredana told him about her friends, including Elena and her friend Isabella. She noticed his expression change, his eyes staring into the distance. "Earth to Biagio."

He smiled. "Sorry. I was thinking about my work. So, where were we?" His lips pressed onto hers, even hungrier this time, his hands touching her breasts and circling her nipples. He pulled away again. "Why don't we go to my car for a bit more privacy?"

Loredana swallowed. It was awfully soon, but she was hungry for this guy and didn't want to wait. She deserved a bit of fun. "Sure, but I should let my friends know."

He shook his head. "No need. We'll only be gone a little while. I'd like some alone time with you, that's all."

"Okay." They headed out of the disco and he put his arm around her shoulder as she braved the evening cold. His car was a short walk away and she'd be comfortable within the confines of his car. He swung open the rear door of his car, then wrapped his arms around her and kissed her deeply. She hopped into the back seat, and he crawled in after her. He lifted up her dress and pulled down her panties, flicking his finger inside her and probing until she climaxed. His hands touched her everywhere, and she was excited beyond belief. He certainly knew how to please a woman, and she relished the time. After all, she was a woman with needs in spite of not knowing him at all. Any other woman would definitely not go this far with a guy, but she was different.

He moved off her and leaned forward towards his glove compartment. He pulled out a condom. Then Loredana took off his pants and placed it on him. She was wet with arousal, and his fingers probed her again. He leaned on top of her and teased her nipples with his tongue. He planted kisses across her chest and stomach. Then he entered her, and it was the most exquisite thing she'd ever felt. She panted and moved against him, brushing her hands through his wavy hair and moaning in pleasure. With a harder thrust, Loredana climaxed along with him. As they caught their breath, Biagio abruptly moved away from her.

He smiled at Loredana. "That was amazing. You're amazing!"

"Thanks. You're not so bad yourself."

"Can I ring you or visit you at work?" he asked.

Loredana nodded. "Of course." She gave him the address of her work and her home phone number.

"I have something I have to do, so how about I give you a call soon."

Loredana felt a rush of excitement. He might or might not be her one true love, but she was definitely in lust. "I'll talk to you soon."

She opened the car door, waited for him to enter the driver's door, then waved at him. As she made her way back to the disco, she wondered if he'd actually call. She knew he probably wouldn't. It was just a bit of fun, even if he didn't call her.

When she met with her group of friends, Francesco and Elena looked worried. Loredana scowled. She didn't need to be judged. She'd had enough of that from her own parents. Francesco's two friends, who must've just arrived, stared at her too. She knew that one of them had a crush on her but she wasn't interested.

Francesco grabbed her by the arm. "Where the hell were you? We were worried."

She shrugged. "I just met a guy, that's all."

He looked at her with concern. "You cannot carry on with guys this way, Loredana. You're too easy. There are too many of them that'll take advantage of you, then leave you like discarded rubbish. You have to be careful with these strangers."

Loredana's chest tightened, her hands clenching. "I don't need you to tell me how to live my life. I'm old enough to do what I want. Besides, you're not my papa. I've already got one of those. I don't need another."

Francesco sighed and turned away. Elena watched her with a frown and a reassuring smile. The sad thing was that Francesco was right. She had a weak spot when it came to men, but she couldn't stop herself. It was like an addiction. In spite of that, she sincerely hoped that Biagio would call her or visit at work.

CHAPTER 18
A STRANGE MEETING

Elena dusted around the shop, her mind focused on Francesco and the way he'd looked at her at the disco a few nights ago. Was it her imagination, or did he really have an interest in her romantically?

She cast her mind back to the way his eyes continually flicked back and forth towards her, the way his smiling eyes lit up his face, and how he fixed his gaze on her. The way he pulled up his sleeves to show his tanned and taut muscles, causing her to lose all breath. The way he spoke her name and how his dimples lined his cheeks.

When Elena had caught him staring, he'd suddenly turned back to his friends. He was trying desperately to fight her off, but why? Why didn't he make a move when she was free and available? It wasn't like her father was around and Francesco was worried about him. She was in a new city with new opportunities, but he failed to take advantage of that.

The ringing of the doorbell broke her reverie, and Elena turned to face the door. It was Loredana, accompanied by a man with a crooked nose and the darkest eyes she had ever seen. A strange feeling settled over her chest as they walked in with their heads thrown back in laughter. He was the man Francesco had spoken to her about at the disco. The man she'd walked off with. A mere stranger.

"Hey, gorgeous! I'd like you to meet Biagio. He's a friend of mine."

Biagio drew back and frowned. "Is that all I am to you, my dearest Loredana? A friend?"

She chuckled. "Well, okay then. A friend with benefits."

"Hmmm," he said. Biagio turned to Elena and held out his hand. "Good to meet you, Elena." His hand was cold and firm, and he had a magnetic presence. She could easily understand how Loredana would get taken in by him in the dark of night.

"Hi there," Elena said.

Loredana pulled him by the hand and led him out back. "We'll be in the back. Will you be okay here for a while?"

Elena nodded.

She watched them scurry out back, Biagio's hands squeezing Loredana's buttocks, then pushing her ahead. He looked familiar to her, but she couldn't place him. Yet she had the strangest feeling that this man was a womaniser and not someone you could trust. How could she make that judgement when she'd never met the man before? Maybe because her own sister had been through difficulties with men and now she was facing her own challenges. Or maybe they'd crossed paths somewhere before, too briefly for her to remember.

The door swung open and Francesco walked in. He carried a money bag in one hand and drew his other hand through his hair.

"Hey, Elena. I wasn't meant to be coming in today, but I thought I'd get out the takings and make a deposit at the bank."

He flicked open the cash register and took out the liras, stashing them inside the bag while Elena stood back with her arms crossed.

"So, did you have a good time at the disco?"

Elena wanted a reaction out of Francesco, so she said, "Sure did. My friend Isabella did too, and kind of thinks you're handsome. Maybe you two should go out."

Francesco looked up from the cash register. He looked at her strangely. She couldn't make out what he was thinking, but his eyes had darkened. She thought he might rise to her bait. Instead he said, "So have you had any more surprise deliveries?"

She shook her head. "Nothing at all. Hopefully the joker has stopped."

Elena heard moans and groans from the back, and Francesco closed the cash register. He was about to rush out back, but Elena pulled him by the arm. "Leave it. That's Loredana's new boyfriend. You go, and I'll deal with it."

"No, that's forbidden. They shouldn't be carrying on like that in a place of business. Why would she bring him here when she has to work?" He sighed. "Listen, why don't you go home, and I'll put a stop to this. He'll be leaving and Loredana will be here on her own. I think you've worked long enough."

She shrugged. "Are you sure?"

He nodded.

"Okay."

She grabbed her bag from the corridor shelf near the staff room but avoided looking out back. The moans were getting louder and she felt her cheeks flush.

As she was leaving, she saw Francesco walk out back in a huff. What the hell was he going to do to the guy? She'd hate to be on Francesco's bad side.

***

Elena lay on her bed on her stomach, writing in her creative writing book. She had started a story based on the unrequited love of a man and a woman. It probably reflected her own life with Francesco, but she would get all her feelings into the book.

She put down her pen and lay on her back, stretching out her arms. She yawned and briefly closed her eyes. It was all quiet. Nunziata was out so she had peace. No nagging, no criticisms, and no orders to do a bunch of chores.

A light tap on her window jolted her from the bed. She approached the window but saw nothing. Then the telephone rang outside her bedroom. She walked out and picked it up. The sound of raspy breathing at the other end unsettled her.

"Who is this?" Silence. "Who are you?"

She'd barely hung up the phone when it rang again. Elena picked it up slowly. "Hello."

What she heard this time was chilling. "Get the fuck out of Milan, you bitch." Then the line went dead.

She swallowed and felt her hand shake as she placed the receiver back in its cradle. The phone rang again but she let it ring and scurried back to her room. Elena ripped out a loose piece of paper from her notebook and started writing notes on everything that was happening to her. She would take it to the police the minute she'd documented everything. This had gone on long enough.

CHAPTER 19
AN INCIDENT

Elena sluggishly walked towards the Questura di Milano. A weathered, dull-brown, flat-topped building with rectangular windows, the police station, looked drab and old. The officers exiting the building wore dark blue jackets and light blue trousers, each with a thin purple stripe. She watched as two police officers entered a light blue car with a white stripe and "Polizia" written on the side.

She reached the arched entrance, and took a breath when stepping inside the police station, wondering if she was doing the right thing. Behind the counter, a man with a multitude of wrinkles and a paunch stood with crossed arms and bore his eyes deep into her soul. Maybe he was suspicious of everyone. Maybe he'd been on the job for far too long and failed to trust anyone.

Police officers stared at her as they exited and entered the building. The darkness and cold of the spacious interior made her hands feel numb.

The man behind the counter cleared his throat and clasped his hands. "How can I help you, Miss?"

She was pleasantly surprised by his soft voice, a sharp contrast to his body language. "I need to speak to a police officer about a situation."

He exhaled. "Excuse me."

"I'm being harassed by someone. I've had threatening phone calls, notes, and someone tapping on my window at home. I need help to stop them."

The policeman pursed his lips and shook his head. "Unless there's an actual crime, Miss, we cannot help you."

Elena's chest tightened. "What do you mean?"

"Well, has this person hurt you physically or tried to kill you?"

She shook her head. "But he's been threatening me verbally, and I know I'm being followed. I don't feel safe, even in my own home. You have to stop him."

"Him, Miss?"

Elena had never considered that a woman could be involved. "Well, I'm only assuming."

"Miss, I think what you need to do is make sure you don't go out alone and watch your surroundings. If you feel that he's going to hurt you in any way, then give us a call. But there's been no crime committed here."

"But I don't feel safe. I'm being terrorised."

He turned away a moment. "And that is not a crime here in Italy. We have no such laws in Milan, so now you know." He looked at his watch. "I'm afraid I have a pressing appointment, so if you don't mind, you'll need to leave."

Elena drew her eyebrows together. With drooped shoulders, she walked outside and felt her body shake. She closed her eyes for a moment and bowed her head. What was she going to do now? How could terrorising people not be against the law? It should've been a crime, but the law didn't acknowledge it. Surely those who harassed others most likely resorted to crimes eventually? She didn't think this person had any plans to stop anytime soon, and she hoped he wouldn't resort to more drastic measures.

Elena made her way home on the bus and stepped off into her street. She ambled but felt strangely uneasy as she unlocked the front door. She froze at the sight before her. Nunziata was lying on the floor, rubbing her temple as if she had a headache. The right corner of her face sported a bluish-red bruise and she moaned as she pushed herself up into a sitting position.

Elena rushed towards her. "What happened?" She laid an arm on the older woman's shoulder but Nunziata pushed it away.

"Some strange man wearing a mask. He forced himself inside and asked to see you."

Elena drew back. "What?"

Nunziata closed her eyes briefly as if fighting her pain. "He came in and said he was an old friend of yours." She moaned in pain. "Said that I shouldn't trust you in my own home." She cleared her throat. "He said that you're very easy with men."

"What was this guy's name?"

Nunziata shrugged. "He didn't say when I asked him, but he seemed to know who you were. He even described you, so you must know him." She pursed her lips. "But if you are prostituting yourself or taking drugs, you can leave right now. I won't put up with that in my home."

Elena shook her head. Now this person was playing at games to affect her residency. What more was the creep planning to do? "Check my room. There are no drugs, okay? It's obviously someone who's probably seen me, but I don't have any friends like that. None that would assault a woman."

"If I find out you're lying to me, you are out of here."

Elena decided to tell her the whole story. "I have something to tell you, and that's where I was earlier today. I went to the police, but they say they can't do a damn thing about it."

Elena went on to mention how she'd been terrorised these past months. Throughout the story, Nunziata frowned as if suspending an opinion. When Elena had finished, the older woman clasped her hands over her heart and said, "Oh my goodness! Are you okay?"

"I am, but don't you think we should report this to the police? This guy must be the same one who's threatening me."

Nunziata stayed silent. "Ah, the police. They won't do any damn thing about this. They're useless and couldn't even save my poor Federico."

Elena waited for more, but nothing came. "Who is Federico?"

Nunziata turned away, a tear falling down her flushed face. Elena helped her up and, together, they entered the kitchen and sat down. Elena clasped her hands and waited. Nunziata sat with her head bowed. Then she swallowed and lifted her gaze to Elena's. "Okay, I will tell you about my husband. My Federico."

CHAPTER 20
DISCLOSURE

Nunziata cleared her throat. Hands shaking, she fixed her gaze on Elena. If only she hadn't treated this poor girl like the enemy. She wasn't the enemy. The only enemy was herself and her anger over life. This poor girl was trying to make a life for herself and here she was tarnishing that. She felt comfortable telling her story in Elena's company.

"My Federico and my twenty-year-old son died in a car accident ten years ago. The police were chasing after my husband because he had stolen some jewellery from a Milan store. They chased him until—until his car wrapped around a tree after he lost control."

Elena gave her a reassuring gaze. "I am so sorry for your loss, Nunziata."

She took a breath and carried on. "He was a gambler and alcoholic, but I still loved my Federico." She fought back the tears. "I tried to get him some help. I asked the police if they knew of anyone who could help him, but they just told me he was a criminal and would pay for his thieving. He'd done it a few times so he could pay gambling debts, but the police refused to believe that he was a troubled man."

Elena leaned forward. "How was he troubled?"

Nunziata had only ever told her story to a few of her old friends back in Laurino but none of her new friends in Milan knew. It was time to tell her story again. "He witnessed a man getting stabbed at his building site where he worked. This man was stabbed multiple times in the throat, in the stomach, and in the chest by an older man. My Federico was a courageous man, so he tried to stop him, but the madman went after him and stabbed him in the right eye. He became unconscious and eventually lost that eye." Nunziata felt her nerves pulling in her chest, her eyes closing for a moment. The silence was almost calming. "He wasn't the same after that experience. He was having nightmares, flashbacks, paranoia, and even became verbally aggressive towards my son, Domenico, and to me. I asked him to see a doctor, but he refused, saying he didn't want to relive the experience. Then I tried getting the police to force him to get help but they only planned to lock him away instead of being admitted into a hospital. It is bad today with the police, but in those days, it was much worse."

Elena tilted her head. "How did your son get to be in the car?"

Nunziata couldn't believe their bad luck. Sometimes fate stepped in, and maybe that was her Domenico's time in life. He wasn't called to this life to live a long time. It was God's will that he left this earth earlier than she had wanted. "Domenico wanted to take his father to see a doctor and get a referral to a psychiatrist, but I told him that his father wasn't feeling well and refused to go. He wasn't. He was lying in bed and getting over his drunken state from the night before. I couldn't drive, but Domenico was adamant about at least taking him to see the doctor for the referral. He'd become too distant from Domenico and me after the incident at work, and didn't seem to care about anything. He didn't care about much else but his drinking and gambling."

She laid a hand on her chest, offering herself comfort. It was always a challenge telling her story, but she needed to make Elena understand. "Anyway, I was washing the clothes and doing housework when I heard the front door slam. I went to see what happened when I noticed that Federico was being dragged into the car by Domenico. I rushed out of the house, but I noticed the police had just arrived. They told me they needed to speak to Federico about a burglary at a local jewellery store. Domenico must've noticed the police coming earlier in their cars and tried to make a dash for it. I think he was trying to protect my Federico from the police. He honestly thought my Federico needed specialist help. At least a doctor could say he wasn't in his right mind when he stole that jewellery."

Nunziata remembered how she'd tried to call out after Domenico but he'd already driven off in a frenzy while the police chased after him. "As I couldn't do anything but hope that Domenico would stop for the police, I prayed that he would not drive like a raving lunatic just because he needed to get away from the police. So I waited and waited but both of them never came home. The police came back to my house a couple of hours later to give me the news. Both Federico and Domenico were killed instantly in the car." She let the tears fall. "He must have been driving too fast to hit that tree the way he did. If only I'd stopped Domenico from leaving to face the police. If only he hadn't driven like a madman. They'd both be with me right now." She shook her head. "After what happened with Domenico in Laurino, I couldn't believe he'd have worse luck. That was the reason we came to Milan."

Nunziata wondered why the police couldn't have been more helpful and why they had to go chasing them as if they were serial killers. They weren't crazy.

Elena reached out and patted Nunziata's hand. "What do you mean? What happened in Laurino?"

Nunziata wondered whether to tell her about the fifteen-year-old boy who hurt her son.

"He got involved in drugs in Laurino, and the very person who got him into drugs was someone I could never set my eyes on again."

Elena shook her head. "I'm sorry. I can't imagine what you went through. Are you okay?"

Nunziata shrugged. "I am a strong woman. Don't worry. We have no control over destiny, and that was my family's destiny." She was interrupted by a knock at the door. Rising from the chair, she said, "Are you expecting anyone, Elena? I'm not."

Elena said, "No. Would you like me to see who it is?"

Nunziata smiled. "I'll come with you."

They both headed to the door. Elena's eyes widened and her cheeks flushed as she drew back from a handsome man at the door. Nunziata watched as he greeted Elena with a handshake. She knew that man. Why did he look so familiar?

It eventually came to her. This was Francesco. He was older now, but now that she'd placed him, she could still see the boy who had done errands for her husband in Laurino. The same one who had got her son into drugs. She pressed her hands to her sides to keep from slapping him. What was he doing in Milan?

CHAPTER 21
INTIMATE

Francesco turned to the woman he recognised. His heart got caught in his throat and his vocal cords knotted. His feet planted themselves firmly on the floor as if he couldn't budge from his position. What in hell was this woman doing here? She would spoil everything and then where would he be? Out of Elena's life so fast he wouldn't know what had happened.

For a moment, he dared to hope she wouldn't recognise him, but by the look in her eyes, she seemed to know exactly who he was. He had to do something before she spilled the beans, and fast. They hadn't made peace after he moved to Milan, and he hadn't seen her for all those years. She couldn't know how much he'd changed, and the fire in her eyes showed that she had still lived in the past and was about to make trouble.

He smiled at Elena and nodded at Nunziata. "Ladies." He turned to Elena. "Can I have a glass of water?"

Elena watched him closely, as if she was trying to figure him out. Then she turned and disappeared into the kitchen. The air was thick with tension as this older woman's gaze seemed to burn in his chest. He had to put out that fire before Elena knew the truth.

Nunziata headed towards him and shook her head. "Is it really you, Francesco? Is it you?"

He nodded. "Please don't say anything to Elena. I'd like to tell her things about my old life in due course. She doesn't need to know about my past."

Nunziata's chin quivered. "Oh, how you hurt my son." She clenched her fists. "Not only that, but how you used to taunt the girls in the village and how your father—" She turned to Elena who walked in with a tall glass of water.

"Is everything okay here? You guys look like you know each other."

Nunziata cleared her throat and touched her neck, her fingers lingering on the hollow in her throat. She stared at Francesco as if wondering how he could imagine she'd keep his past hidden from Elena.

Maybe Elena did have a right to know, but not all his sins were in his past. There was what he was doing to her right now. If he told her the truth, she'd hate him. She'd leave her job at the shop and he'd never see her again. He was falling for her, but he couldn't make the mistake of getting too close. He had too many secrets. It wasn't right to deceive her this way but what choice did he have? One day, he'd summon the courage to say no to his father. He'd show the old man how tough and strong he really was. Not the wimp he used to be back in the day.

Elena's touch on his arm jolted him back to the present.

Nunziata's eyes flashed at him. "I think you need to tell Elena the truth. Or so help me God, I will." She walked away in a huff.

Elena turned to Francesco. "What is she talking about?"

He shrugged. "Can we go for a walk? I'll tell you the story."

Elena nodded, then opened the front door. Francesco smelled the lavender perfume she wore. He liked it. He liked the way she drew a slender hand through her chestnut hair whenever she was nervous. Like now. She bit her lip as they walked outside and headed along the footpath in the direction of the shops. Cars emitted fumes as they drove past. Another driver beeped someone in front, then came within an inch of hitting the car. A woman pushing her baby in a pram smiled at them as she walked past. Did she think they were a couple? Was it the chill in the air that made him shiver or was it his own past?

As Elena's shoulder brushed against his, he felt an overwhelming urge to hold and kiss her. Would it be so bad to kiss her at least once before he told her the truth? If he told her the truth now, she would never speak to him again. Maybe he could tell her part of the truth. Just enough to keep the old woman quiet. He was wrestling with himself when Elena cut through the silence. "Something disturbing has been going on." She explained about the threats she'd been having. "I visited the police, but they can't do anything." She explained what the policeman had said.

The thought of someone threatening her made Francesco want to punch something. "That's so unfair. This guy could seriously hurt you and they wouldn't care. It's so typical of this country. All these police are corrupt, and my papa's one of them."

Elena's head spun so fast he thought her head might drop off. "Your papa's a policeman? Where?"

He shook his head, deciding to tell her part of the truth. "In Laurino." He waited for her reaction.

She tilted her head and peered into the distance. "You never told me you were from Laurino. I never met you there."

Francesco swallowed. "I left ten years ago and stayed with a friend until I could afford my own place. I know Nunziata from there, and—"

"And what? What happened?"

Francesco's heart beat fast. He could do this. He had to do this for the sake of his sanity. Besides, he wanted Elena to trust him.

Francesco found a bench and headed towards it. He sat, and Elena followed suit, the proximity of her body to his causing a flutter in his heart.

"But you would've been very young then. How old were you, and why did you leave?"

"I was fifteen at the time, and I left because I didn't get along with my papa. He used his macho pride on me, and his fists, and I was sick of it."

"And the scar? Was that your father too?"

Francesco felt queasy, remembering the day his father had punished him simply because he'd gone to his friend's house down the road without his permission. "My papa hit me with the steel part of his belt and gave me this scar. He used it a few times on me." He felt his throat dry up.

Elena squeezed his shoulder. "I'm so sorry." A tear rolled down her cheek.

Francesco laid his hand on top of hers and gave her a reassuring smile. He soldiered on. "And I knew Nunziata's son Domenico. I introduced him to this acquaintance who was into the drug scene, only because I was helping a friend of mine get out of his debt. He said that if he introduced me to another sucker who'd sell drugs for him that he'd let my friend go free." He drew a shaky hand through his hair. "You don't know how sick this guy was. I felt guilty doing that to her son, but I had to help out my friend. He owed these drug dealers money and needed to get out of that scene. He's free and clear now, but I had to make a choice back then."

Elena's chin quivered. She held her index finger and thumb under it and stared into the distance, saying nothing. He wondered what she was thinking and if she was judging him for the past. If only she'd say something. Instead, she took a deep breath and turned to face him, her eyes unreadable. He had to find a way to show Elena that, while he'd made a lot of mistakes in the past, he wasn't about to repeat them. He was a stupid teenager at the time.

"Elena, are you okay? What are you thinking?"

She shook her head, as if to rid it of unwelcome thoughts. "He was older than you at the time, so don't blame yourself. At least he got out of it by coming to Milan. But then he got killed in that accident."

He nodded. "I heard about that. Poor Nunziata. I need to apologise to her. Make her understand that what I did was for good reason. I had no other choice."

"She will. In her own time."

They stared at each other for a few moments. Those lips of hers enticed him, and he found himself getting lost in her eyes. Elena leaned in towards him and licked her lips. He cupped her chin in his hand, tilting her head upward. His face inched closer to hers. He had to kiss her. He couldn't fight his feelings for her any longer. She had to be his, and he'd deal with the consequences later.

As he leaned in further, he brushed her lips lightly with his. She kissed him back, and his whole body tingled with arousal. His breathing felt laboured. He pulled away from her. "I care about you so much, Elena. You are so beautiful." He feathered her cheek with the back of his fingers and moved in for another kiss. This time his lips fell over hers hungrily and deeply, their tongues intertwining and dancing as they wrapped their arms around each other. He stroked the strands of her hair and tantalised her across her neck, then kissed her again and plunged his tongue even deeper. Elena moaned and arched her back against his hand.

Then something rustled nearby, followed by the sound of shattering glass from the house behind them.

Francesco pulled away from Elena and rose from the bench. His eyes roamed but he saw no one who could have smashed the front window of the house. Luckily, no one was home or they'd probably blame him and Elena.

"Let's go, Elena. Someone just smashed that window, and I'm not about to endanger your life with some weirdo around."

Elena swallowed. "Sure, let's go."

After saying an awkward goodbye to Elena, he noticed that as she swung open the door, a scrunched-up note lay on the ground. *That wasn't there before*, he thought, as she bent to pick it up. *What could it be?* He waited until the door closed behind her. Then, satisfied that she was safe, he made his way to his car and drove off.

CHAPTER 22
PARTIAL TRUTH

Elena bent down and picked up the note. She unfolded it and read the scrawl, saying, *"Francesco is not the man for you. You need to leave Milan."*

She crossed her arms and pondered the note. When would this person harassing her let up? It got to the point that she avoided leaving the house. How did this person even know Francesco unless he was watching them and making up silly stories? He must've been the one who smashed the window and hurt Nunziata. It couldn't all be a coincidence. What did he want with her? Her whole life, she'd lived in a small Italian village, and she'd never made enemies there. She'd made a few friends since coming to the big city, but only one person had shown himself to be hostile. Thinking it through, Elena was sure it was Angelo terrorising her, but how dangerous was he?

Shaking away her worry and walking to her bedroom, she turned to more beautiful thoughts. An image of Francesco's handsome face flashed before her. The way he'd stroked her cheek, stared hungrily into her eyes, and gently touched the small of her back. Even the way his masterful tongue tantalised her and kept her wanting more. She was falling hard for Francesco, but she sensed he was still holding back. Something unspoken still stood between them. She couldn't put her finger on it, but she could tell Francesco was still hiding something. She was determined to find out what.

She lay back against her pillow and looked up at the ceiling. Turning to the window, she saw drops of rain falling against the glass. Luckily, she was staying inside today and planned to do some writing in her notebook and fashion designs in her sketch pad. It was early days yet, but pretty soon, she'd need to create a collection for a new portfolio. She smiled at the thought.

A knock at her door broke her reverie. "Come in."

Nunziata hobbled inside, still appearing to be in pain. "I just wanted to talk to you about Francesco. Did he tell you that we knew each other? I didn't want to lie about that."

Elena rose from her bed and sat at the edge. Nunziata grabbed a chair from the desk and sat across with her palms clasped together. "He mentioned knowing you in Laurino. I didn't even know he lived there until today."

Nunziata cleared her throat and looked past her. "I just thought I'd tell you to be careful with him. Did he tell you about my son?"

Elena's chest tightened. "He told me about Domenico. He said he had no choice. He was saving his friend."

"A likely excuse, but my Domenico got into drugs because of Francesco's other friend."

Elena drew back. "No, that guy was just someone dangerous. He didn't want to risk his friend's life."

Nunziata chuckled, but there was no humour in it. "So he chose to risk my son's life instead."

Elena couldn't believe what she was hearing. "Your son was twenty years old, so he had a choice too. Not all of the blame goes on Francesco. You have to let this go, Nunziata. He's not the way you say he is. He's a good person."

Nunziata ignored her comment. "Back in his day, he was a ladies' man. A charmer. I don't want to see you get hurt."

Elena felt nauseous. Was he only using her for one thing? Did he really care about her or was she no more than an interesting challenge for now? "But we're only friends. I work with him, and he's my boss. That's all."

Nunziata pursed her lips. She stared at the ground in silence and shifted her feet as if she was itching to say something more.

"What's going on?" Elena said. "I mean, you haven't seen Francesco since he was fifteen. That was ten years ago, and right now, I'd say he's more mature and pretty much a man. He would've changed since then, don't you think?"

She shrugged. "Maybe. Maybe not. Just be careful."

Elena was curious. "What are you not telling me?"

"Look, he's had a hard life and more than his fair share of trauma, so take it easy with him. I saw the way he looked at you. With lust in his eyes. I'm worried. You're young, impressionable, and innocent. Francesco is experienced and more knowing in the ways of the world. Don't let him make you grow up too quickly."

She chuckled. "You're talking about sex, aren't you?"

Nunziata blushed and turned away. "Look, he used to flirt with many girls in Laurino and broke many hearts. His father was a problem too, but it's not my business to get into his personal life. If you're friends, then he should tell you those things. But maybe just keep your relationship friendly. Not beyond that. I don't want to be picking up the pieces."

Elena didn't respond. She shifted her posture and turned away, thinking that her relationship with Francesco was none of Nunziata's business. It wasn't like Nunziata was her mother. She was simply offering her hospitality for the next few years. That didn't mean she got to tell Elena how to live her life. Besides, it was too late not to get in too deep with Francesco. She was starting to develop real feelings for the man.

Nunziata got up and placed the chair back by the desk. "I'll see you later."

Elena nodded. She rested back on her bed and thought about Francesco. If only she could find out what was really going on with him.

CHAPTER 23
TAUNTING

Valentina clapped her hands. "Attention everyone! Attention! Today's class is exciting to say the least. We are going to draw on further exploration of fabrics and designs." She paced around the room, looking at students square in the eye. "I'd like to give you a taste of how to start thinking about a portfolio to create a collection. We're going to look at matching a design with a fabric, then I'd like you to peer critique. Each of you will be commenting on each other's rough design and write a report." She rubbed her hands together. "Okay people. Choose your fabrics and create your design."

Elena nodded towards Isabella, who smiled. "You and me are partners, Isabella."

Nodding, she said, "Sure. Let's head over to that table. There's more variety of fabrics over there."

They scurried over to the table, and Elena almost bumped into Angelo, who smirked and made his way towards the opposite table. Elena dug into an array of fabrics, feeling the thickness of the heavy knit fabrics, tartan, synthetics, and polyester. Finally, she picked up a sample of a crème chiffon material. She had an idea for a chiffon evening dress and was excited to start sketching. Oh, the images running around in her mind right now was mind-boggling, and she couldn't wait. This was her ultimate dream; to start creating and apply her creativity and talents for the world to see.

Heading over to the design table, Elena took out her sketch pad and designed an image from her mind. She remembered seeing a similar version of the dress and had got the idea to add more finesse and style to it. She wanted it to look regal, stylish, and elegant, a dress that would be made on a haute couture basis. A particular market that could afford a more stylish evening design. She also had an idea for a tweed coat dress that could be her next design. Valentina was doing a good job of preparing the class for their future collection towards the end of their course.

As Elena bowed her head to draw, she sketched lightly with a pencil to outline a gathered texture with a round neck, short sleeves, a fitted tight waist, and a length down to the ankles. A thicker silk fabric would be attached to the back of the dress to create another dress down from the waist for a butterfly effect. It would look amazing when she was done.

Isabella propped her chin on one hand and watched Elena work. Elena was almost finished but Isabella looked dumbfounded as if struggling with an idea. Elena turned towards her and put down her pencil.

"So, what kinds of fabrics do you like, Isabella?"

She squinted. "I like tartan, knit fabrics, and light cottons but I don't have a clue about a design. I think I'm out of my depth here."

Elena gave her a reassuring smile. "Close your eyes and relax for a minute. I'm sure an idea will come to you." She paused. "Maybe think about a design you've seen that you liked. You could always adapt that design to fit your style. Give it a try, but close your eyes and don't get distracted by the other students."

Isabella turned away from her. She closed her eyes and held a pencil in her shaky hand. Rather than looking relaxed, she looked tense.

Elena felt Angelo's dark eyes in her direction. He winked and blew her a kiss. She shook her head in disgust. When would he leave her alone and take the hint? More and more, she was beginning to think he might be the one terrorising her. She certainly wouldn't put it past him, not by the way he was acting.

Once the rest of her classes ended, Elena stepped outside the building and waved goodbye to Isabella, who had eventually come up with a design, showcasing a cotton shift dress that Elena commented on positively. She got a good rating and report from Isabella too, and was excited to try her design on a dress form.

Ambling towards the bus, Elena felt a hand tugging her shoulder. She turned to see Angelo grinning at her. It was all she could do not to cringe.

"Let's go have a coffee," he said. "I'd like us to talk."

"No, I have to go. I'm going to miss my bus."

Something in his eyes shifted. He bit his lip, bowed his head, and swore to himself. Elena felt suddenly cold. He didn't let go of her shoulder, and his nails dug hard into her skin. He pulled her towards him, and continued to press hard into both shoulders. She lifted her hands and pushed him away, but he wouldn't budge. She was no match for his strength.

"You're at least giving me a chance," he said. "I'm tired of being judged without people getting to know me. Come on, let's go. Give me a chance. One coffee, that's all."

Elena saw desperation in his eyes, but she refused to feel sorry for him. He was a bully, and right now he was forcing his strong hands onto her body to propel her forward. Eventually he let go and she hurried in the opposite direction. Angelo chased her, then grabbed her from behind with an angry laugh. She noticed passers-by watching with curiosity, but Angelo made out as if he was having fun with her. He turned her around and held her around the waist. Then he leaned in and planted a kiss on her lips. She tried to push him away with her hands, but he didn't move.

"Let me go! Please let me go!"

Before he could answer, his body jerked backward, then sprawled to the ground. Another set of strong arms grabbed her hand and shoved her behind a familiar figure. It was Francesco.

Eyes blazing, he jabbed a finger towards Angelo. "You touch her again, and I'll kill you. Do you hear me, you creep?"

Angelo pushed himself up from the ground and stared at Francesco hard. "I wasn't even hurting her. We were only having a conversation, man. I'm not the creep here."

Francesco stared back, his hands on his hips. "Get out of here. You had no right to kiss her when she hates your guts."

"And what? You think she's going to kiss you? The macho dude? The one who thinks he's God's gift to women? I think Elena needs a man with more substance, more experience."

Francesco chuckled. "And I guess that man is you, is it? The man of substance?"

Angelo nodded. "She hasn't even given me a chance." His eyes turned to Elena in desperation. "Given *us* a chance."

"Please go, Angelo. I'm not interested, so please accept that."

The dark cloud that spread across his face sent chills down her legs. He muttered something under his breath, glared at Francesco, then, as if appearing to calm himself down, sauntered off. His back was a little too stiff for the saunter to be believable.

Francesco faced her and quickly checked her body for injuries. "Are you okay? Did he hurt you?"

Elena shook her head, fighting back tears. "No, I'm fine. Thanks for helping me."

His eyes darkened further as he held her arm. "Come on. I'll drive you home." He shook his head. "I saw him kiss you too, but I know you tried to stop him."

She wondered what Francesco was doing in this part of Milan when his shop was on the other side. Was it just a coincidence that he had come to her in the nick of time?

CHAPTER 24
A DOUBLE DATE

A week later, Elena answered the door to Francesco. Luckily for him, Nunziata wasn't home. He looked dashing in fitted black pants, a white silk buttoned-up shirt and fine Italian leather shoes. He had stubble that enhanced his good-looks. Since their kiss, he hadn't brought up his feelings. He acted as if the kiss had never happened. Maybe he felt it was a mistake. Elena had no idea where she stood with Francesco.

Elena smiled and locked the door behind her. She followed him to his car parked nearby and sat in the passenger seat. Her stomach tingled, and she was aware of his eyes following her legs when her floral dress lifted above her knees. With her right hand, she pressed down her dress and looked away, feeling her face redden. Oh, how she longed for him to touch her. Francesco, though, had kept his distance again. Her fists tightened. Why didn't he tell her exactly what was on his mind? Why the secrecy?

Elena forced her hands open and drew a fringe away from her eyes. "So where did Loredana say we were meeting?"

Francesco cleared his throat, his eyes focused on the road ahead. "A popular restaurant called La Pobbia. It's about twenty minutes away. They make classic Milanese food, and have been around for more than a hundred years. I think you should like it."

Elena nodded. "What do you think of Loredana's boyfriend?"

He shrugged. "I don't know him well enough to have an opinion. What about you?"

Elena sensed he wasn't being honest. "I think he's a bit intense. Kind of possessive of Loredana, but she seems to like him."

He nodded but stayed silent. He was in that detached mode again, and all she wanted to do was take hold of his hand and stroke it. What was going on with him? She hated how he was both hot and cold with her.

Francesco turned up the music on his radio as if he wanted silence, so she stayed quiet. It wasn't like Francesco had invited her out. It was Loredana who had suggested they both get to know Biagio. Still, even if it was just as a friend, at least she was going out with him. Maybe he'd eventually open up. She was determined to speak her mind when he was in a better mood. Now wasn't the time.

When they finally arrived, he parked in front of the restaurant. Elena exited the car and hugged herself, wrapping her jacket tighter around her. Francesco touched the small of her back and led her towards the entrance. Her cheeks flushed, and her knees suddenly felt weak and wobbly. His touch created fire in her body.

Francesco met with a waiter who showed them to the seating area. Elena enjoyed the dark and romantic ambience—the big fireplace, shelves of bottles lining the back wall, cosy couches, an elegant set of antique chairs surrounding adorned tables, low-lit lamps around the room, and signs that showed other parts of the restaurant. There appeared to be other rooms, possibly for privacy or for functions and events.

Once they were seated in their chairs with Francesco beside her, he looked up to wave towards Loredana and Biagio, who made their way towards them.

Loredana leaned in and kissed both Elena and Francesco. "Thanks for coming, guys. It's such a gorgeous place, isn't it?"

Elena nodded. "So cosy."

"Elena, Francesco," Biagio said as he shook hands with Francesco and then Elena. His hand felt heavy in hers, and he wore a grim expression.

Elena peered through a window that overlooked a garden. She turned back to the others only to notice Francesco staring at her. Ignoring the stomach flutter, Elena watched a waiter hand out menus, then glanced through hers and ignored Francesco, not wanting to show her discomfort.

"What do you recommend?" Elena asked.

Loredana smiled. "The cabbage rolls and risotto dishes are to die for. Even the boiled meats are good, but choose whatever you fancy."

Biagio touched Loredana's shoulder. "How about we start with boiled meats to share?" He looked up at the others.

Francesco said, "Fine with me. We can try a few dishes out and share them. Then have an individual main dish if we're still hungry."

Biagio nodded. "Sounds good."

"Oh, I definitely have to have the hot zabaglione later," Loredana said. "You too, Elena."

"Maybe," Elena said.

After the waiter arrived and took their orders of food and wine, Biagio ogled Loredana. He grabbed her by the chin and kissed her hard on the mouth, his tongue playing with her lips. *Oh, why couldn't they get a room already?*

Loredana pushed him away. "Stop it, will you. You're embarrassing me."

"But you look gorgeous enough to eat."

Francesco watched Elena with an appreciative smile. His leg brushed hers and his hand lingeringly touched her knee.

Ignoring her rapid breathing and palpitating heart, Elena turned to Biagio. "So, tell us about yourself. Are you from here?"

Biagio tilted his head as if she'd asked him if he was a serial killer. "No, born and bred in a village in Salerno, but I adore Milan. It has everything you could possibly want."

Elena nodded. "Has your family moved to Milan as well or are you on your own?"

Biagio chuckled. "On my own. I had to get away from my mother, for sure. She was too stifling. My papa died, and I miss him every day."

"Sorry to hear that," Elena said.

"And what do you do, job-wise?" Francesco asked.

Biagio hesitated. "I'm a carpenter, and I have a few properties of my own that I've helped build. I've had obstacles, but I've made some good investments with money. Money's pretty important to me, as I imagine is important to everyone."

"What's with the interrogation, guys? Leave my darling alone," Loredana said.

Biagio chuckled and winked at Loredana. "It's okay. I don't mind answering questions. It's just that I'm not that interesting."

Elena wasn't sure she liked Biagio. He appeared shallow, and Elena wondered what Loredana saw in him. She was obviously attracted to his good looks, but he had the substance—and charisma—of an insect.

CHAPTER 25
MILAN FASHION WEEK

February, 1973

Elena's chest rose, her heart palpitated, and her mouth went dry as she clapped to the beating sounds of an R&B track. It was Milan Fashion Week, and Valentina had invited the students over to these fashion shows to take notes, critique trends, and watch models who would be trying on their own collections.

Valentina had explained how Milan Fashion Week was partially organised by the National Chamber for Italian Fashion, which was a non-profit organisation that marketed Italian fashion and hosted these fashion events and Milan shows. The shows were held twice a year in Milan with both an autumn/winter event in February/March and a spring/summer event in September/October.

She looked over at the elated faces of Loredana and Isabella, whose eyes ogled the women swaggering down the catwalk. They stood alongside the platform as the women strutted the designs of Fendi, Valentino, Dolce & Gabbana, Prada, Gucci, Giorgio Armani, and Roberto Cavalli. One such winter design featured a woman wearing a tight beanie with a red waist-length jacket, fringed pockets, and flared pants. A white bow with a dangling sash was tied around her neck.

The ambience of clicking cameras, the bright spotlights hovering over the models' designer wear, and the layer upon layer of distinct voices filled Elena with adrenaline. Subgroups lingered in corners of the room, whispering about each design and taking notes, staring wide-eyed at the models.

As another woman modelled down the runway, Elena was in awe of the next design that showcased a wintry ash-black fur hooded jacket with its loose sleeves and billowing body. It would definitely keep people warm in Milan's chilly winters. She scribbled down notes in her handy notebook.

"This is amazing, and I love the music," said Loredana.

Isabella nodded. "We're so lucky to be here. Thanks for letting me come with you, Elena. I appreciate it."

Elena touched her on the shoulder and smiled. "Well, this is part of our project at school, so we have to be here. Although I still would've come even if Valentina hadn't invited us. It's got so much energy and fire, and I have so many inspired ideas."

Loredana turned to stare at Elena. "Is Francesco coming? I thought you invited him."

Elena shrugged. "I did, but he said he couldn't make it." Her chest deflated as she thought of the months that had passed since their one kiss. He'd kept his distance.

Loredana rolled her eyes. "You two need to get your act together."

Elena tilted her head. "What do you mean?"

Isabella laughed and turned to her friend. "She means, you and Francesco need to admit how you feel about each other."

Elena swallowed. She'd had no idea that her friends knew what was going on. Was it that obvious? "I wish he'd spoken to me since—" *Oh no, what had she just done?*

Loredana frowned. "Since what?"

Elena looked away, staring up at the next woman, who looked anorexic in a knitted dress. The music blared and Elena bopped to the music and swayed her hands to the music. "Nothing."

Loredana swung her face around. "Look at me, Elena. You're hiding something. Did something happen between you two?"

Elena didn't want the kiss to get out. It could backfire on her, but both Loredana and Isabella were her friends, and they had a right to know. She stood still and turned to them. "Last year, Francesco kissed me, but then he never mentioned it again. He's distanced himself, and I don't know why. Something's holding him back."

Loredana's eyes widened. "Oh my God! That's huge. I knew he liked you." She screwed up her nose. "Why didn't you tell me earlier?"

The music seemed suddenly louder. She tried to shut out the multitude of voices, the light footsteps of the models, and the flashing cameras with the swiftly-moving photographers. "I don't know. I didn't know what it meant so I thought I'd keep it to myself. It's not like we were a couple."

Isabella gave her a reassuring smile. "I'm sorry, Elena. Maybe you should talk to him about the kiss. He might have something going on."

Loredana broke in. "He seems to be on the phone quite a lot, but every time I go into that tea area, he cuts the conversation. There is something going on, but he won't tell me."

"Maybe he's got a secret girlfriend. Or maybe he's married, living a double-life," said Elena, trying to sound nonchalant.

"Ha ha, you are funny," Loredana said.

"Well, what else could it be? These secret phone calls might be the reason he doesn't want me as his girlfriend. I just don't understand why he kissed me in the first place. It wasn't like I made the first move." She felt nauseous. "I really like him, and I miss the closeness we had. Now, he's keeping away for some reason."

Loredana looked up briefly at the catwalk. "I think Isabella's right. You need to have a heart to heart with him."

"Maybe," Elena said. Her mind ruminated about all the possible ways she could avoid talking to him. She had a feeling she was not going to like the recipient of his phone calls. She didn't know if she could handle finding out who the recipient was, but she was sure she couldn't handle letting things go on as they were. Was she falling in love with Francesco?

CHAPTER 26
MISSING

Loredana watched Elena drink her second glass of champagne at the after-party. Isabella had left when the fashion parade ended, and now Loredana's shoulders hunched over in fatigue. As much as she'd found the fashion show enticing, she didn't love it as much as Elena did. Now Elena didn't want to leave. One thing Loredana didn't want to do, and that was to leave her friend alone with all these strangers. Even Elena's fellow students had left.

Luckily, Angelo hadn't come. Elena explained how he'd been harassing her in and out of school, and how last time, Francesco had saved her from his bullying tactics.

Loredana drew a hand through her wispy strands and exhaled. The heels she wore hurt her back, and her entire body was sore from standing.

Elena had taken photographs with some of the designers who had exchanged addresses and planned to get her connected with the fashion world once she finished her course. That wouldn't be for another couple of years, though. Did Elena really think they would even remember her by then? It was all for a show, with the cameras and lights, nothing more. Most likely, empty promises.

Loredana shook her head at a waiter who offered her another drink of champagne. Elena, on the other hand, grabbed the glass. Loredana stretched out her arm, grabbed the glass from Elena, and placed it back on the tray. The man grunted and left, but he seemed to stop offering anyone else drinks. Why were she and Elena so special?

Elena smirked. "Oh, come on! Why can't I have just one more?"

"I think you've had enough. We need to go, and you need to sober up, girl."

¦ Elena flung herself towards Loredana and hugged her unexpectedly. "I love you, Loredana," she said, her words slightly slurred, "but you're being boring. We are at the best after-party Milan has to offer and you want to go home."

"I'm tired, Elena. Come on. Let's head off."

Elena tossed her hair and gave a coquettish grin. "You go, but I'm staying."

At that moment, a young-looking man with stubble had bumped into Loredana and spilled the entire contents of his champagne on her dress.

"I am so sorry," said the man. "I'll pay for the dry-cleaning."

Loredana patted down her dress, feeling cold and sticky. "It's okay. I'll go get cleaned up." The man left, and Loredana made her way to the ladies' room. "I'll go wash up. I won't be long. Just wait for me here, Elena."

"Sure," said Elena. She swayed, standing on unsteady legs.

Loredana turned back to notice how quiet her friend had become; almost sleepy. They were definitely leaving after she cleaned herself. "Wait right here," she repeated.

After she'd dabbed her dress with cold water and dried herself with paper towels, Loredana left and wandered over to their original position. Elena wasn't in there.

Where did she go? I told her to wait for me.

She moved through the crowd, searching for her friend. Other party-goers jostled and pushed her. One of the models even stepped on her foot. She winced but ignored the pain as she headed into the crowds and made space for herself. Elena was nowhere to be found.

She stopped by a couple and asked, "Excuse me have you seen a young girl with long dark brown hair wearing a tight black dress with a low back?"

The couple shook their heads. She asked a few others, but no one had seen Elena. Loredana was beginning to feel sick to her stomach. How could Elena leave without saying goodbye? She was in no fit state to leave on her own.

If she'd headed home, she'd be at the bus stop, so Loredana would go there. Maybe Elena was already on the bus. She wouldn't have taken a taxi, would she? Or maybe she'd met one of those designers who were taking more photographs and having more drinks and food.

Loredana wandered towards the bus stop and waited. Elena wasn't there, but the bus soon came, so Loredana hopped on and headed to Elena's house. Swallowing, she pondered how sleepy Elena had looked all of a sudden. She wondered whether her friend would've had the energy to walk on her own.

Maybe she'd got her energy back and the alcohol had slowly come out of her system. But not in that amount of time. If only she'd waited.

After arriving at Elena's place, Loredana knocked on the door. An older-looking woman answered.

"Can I help you?"

"Yes, hi. I'm a friend of Elena's and was wondering if she got home from the fashion parade. I seemed to have lost her at the after-party."

The woman shook her head, her expression turning grave. "No, Elena is not here." She tilted her head. "Are you Loredana?"

"Yes. She mentioned me?"

"She said that you work together."

Loredana explained the events prior to her going missing. "I'm sure she's with one of her other friends, but I wish I knew where she went. I guess I'll see her tomorrow at the shop."

The woman didn't respond for a moment. She appeared to be in her own dream world. Then, "Of course," she said. "I'm sure she'll be home soon. You go on home, and I will wait up awhile."

Loredana said goodbye and left with a heavy heart. She hoped Elena was okay, and that nothing bad had happened to her. She was an adult after all, even if she was half-drunk. Surely, she'd gotten herself to a safe place?

CHAPTER 27
UNEXPECTED SURPRISE

Francesco had served his last customer of the evening, and the bell over the door had rung for the last time that evening. He displayed the *closed* sign, walked into the staff area, and sank onto the couch.

He couldn't believe he'd made it through the evening. His throat felt dry, and sweat ran down his cheeks. His mind scattered with disturbing and distressing thoughts. Elena! Where was she, and why hadn't she turned up to work? She'd always notified him when she couldn't come in. Although she'd only been absent twice. Today was a different story.

Loredana had recently left the shop, explaining what had happened at the fashion show. Maybe Elena had decided to return to her village; but why wouldn't she say goodbye? Surely, she wouldn't leave without telling anyone, particularly Nunziata.

Maybe she'd simply got home late and wasn't feeling well after last night. She was probably sleeping and had forgotten to ring him at the shop. There had to be a logical explanation.

Francesco's heart broke at the thought of something terrible happening to her. Their kiss came to the forefront of his mind. Her soft skin, her warm and inviting lips, the smoothness and flowery smell of her hair, and the gentle arousal he felt at her closeness and tender moan. He couldn't get her out of his mind ever since that day, but he knew nothing more could come of it. He was not right for her. His family was not right for her. If she ever found out the truth about him, she'd never speak to him again. That he was sure of.

If only he had met Elena under different circumstances. If only she hadn't been so young and from Laurino. He was going mad having her so close and yet so far, and he was surprised she hadn't brought up the kiss. Maybe she didn't feel for him the way he felt about her.

He thought of the way she blushed whenever she felt embarrassed. Of how she played with the strands of her hair and looked so sweet whenever she spoke her mind in a passionate way. She felt strongly about things and enjoyed learning about and researching a variety of topics. They'd had many interesting conversations about a range of issues, and he was surprised by her maturity and depth of knowledge, which was unusual in someone who had lived only in a village.

They'd had amazing times discovering how much they had in common: their love of fashion, their interest in the same movie and book genres, and their love for family and friends. He was mesmerised by her wit and beauty. He couldn't get her out of his mind. Was he falling in love with her? Could it be possible?

He rose from the couch and drew a quaking hand through his hair. He stared out the window and sighed, then grabbed his bag and set off to find her. Surely, she had to be nearby. If she had returned to Laurino, Nunziata would know.

Remembering that she had a late class tonight, Francesco decided to head to the institute. He scurried to his car, almost oblivious to passers-by knocking into him as he rushed headlong in their direction. Storm clouds were brewing, and a pungent smell filled the air. He blocked his nose and rushed on. When finally he reached his car, he got in and screeched away from the kerb.

Parking alongside the front area of the school, he ran into the foyer and bumped into Isabella, who was carrying a pile of books in one hand and a clutch in the other. She drew back and tilted her head.

Francesco's heart somersaulted. If Isabella was at school, where was Elena? He told himself not to panic. She might be in class, or taking a break in the ladies' room. Just because she and Isabella were friends didn't mean they had to be attached at the hip.

He cleared his throat. "Hi, Isabella. I'm looking for Elena. Is she here?"

Isabella shook her head. "No, she didn't come in today. Even the teacher didn't get any call about her absence. She wasn't at work tonight?"

Francesco felt dizzy but contained it. "No, she wasn't." He explained how she'd been missing since the night before and how Loredana was worried about her too. He tried not to think about what it might mean that she hadn't even attended the school that she loved and treasured so much.

Isabella must have seen the tension in his face, because she touched him gently on the forearm and said, "Maybe she's not well or maybe some crisis happened back home. Why don't we go to her house and see if she's there? Her landlady should know something."

Francesco nodded. "Okay, I've got my car out front. Let's go!"

The drive to Elena's house was gruelling for Francesco, a hundred thoughts crushing his head. He turned to Isabella, who was quiet and in her own world, and decided to make conversation.

"So, I understand you went to the fashion show as well."

She nodded. "I did, but I left earlier. I get pretty tired from these social events. There's only so much socialising I can do, and then I like to be alone."

Francesco smiled. "I get it. Too much stimulation and socialising can make anyone sick. You need a balance." He turned onto Elena's street. "Did you see anyone strange hanging around you guys? Anyone acting strangely towards Elena?"

Isabella put her head down and closed her eyes briefly, as if reliving the moment. She turned back to him fully alert. "No, the guys were all busy doing their own thing within their own groups. I couldn't see anyone strange at all." She bowed her head again. "My God, Francesco! What if something terrible happened to her? Should we be calling the police?"

He gave her another reassuring smile. "Not yet. She might be sick at home with the flu. We'll talk to Nunziata, and hopefully she's home."

Isabella nodded. "I hope you're right."

Francesco turned off the engine and took a deep breath. He exited the car and walked around to Isabella, who was shaking all over. He put a gentle hand on her shoulder and walked alongside her to the front door. He knocked on the door and waited for what seemed like hours but was probably more like a minute.

Nunziata opened the door in her dressing gown. She stood wide-eyed. Her face looked more lined than the last time he'd seen her.

She said, "Please tell me that Elena is with you." She stared past them as if Elena was on her way inside. "Where is she?"

Francesco felt a pinch in his stomach, his hands sweating. "Do you mean to tell me that she didn't come home last night?"

Nunziata shook her head. "No, and this morning I noticed that her bed hadn't been slept in." She gave an audible sigh. "Do you mean to tell me she didn't show up for work or school ?"

"No, she didn't." He turned to Isabella. "This is her friend Isabella from school."

Isabella voiced her concerns. "I'm worried that she wasn't at school today. The teacher didn't even hear from her. Elena wouldn't do that, would she? I mean, not tell anyone about being absent?"

"No, she wouldn't. She is a good person with a strong heart. I'm worried," said Nunziata.

Francesco said, "I'm going to the police."

Nunziata nodded. "Fat lot of good they'll do, but you can try."

Francesco had to try something. He felt helpless, and he couldn't lose Elena. Not this way. He hoped she was safe and unhurt, but his heart told him otherwise.

CHAPTER 28
A LOST CAUSE

Francesco held up his hands in desperation, floundering with Elena's situation. He pointed a finger at the policeman, who had stood his ground.

"Listen, like I said. We have more important cases here to deal with."

Francesco rested his hands on the counter then banged them hard against it. "Damn it! This is a woman's life we're talking about. Something bad could've happened to her. Don't you even care?"

"Of course we care," said the policeman. He tugged up his pants with a belt that seemed to need another few notches. "But we've had a lot of cases where we investigated, wasted a lot of resources, and then it ends up that the missing person ran away or left home to live with a boyfriend. I'm sure that's the case here. This Elena woman most likely needed some time out from her responsibilities and is taking a much-needed break. Maybe she's taken a holiday. That's all this is."

Francesco pulled out another card. "Did you know she was being harassed by someone?"

The policeman cleared his throat and turned away, staring at another policeman drinking coffee at his desk. "Sure. She came to tell us, but harassment in Italy is not punishable by law. We only investigate actual crimes."

"But what if this person has escalated? How can you live with yourselves if something happens and you guys did nothing to help? How would that look to whoever's in charge here?"

The policeman took out a notepad and jotted notes. "I need your full statement. We can investigate for a short while, but that's it. It won't be our priority case as you know. We have murderers, thieves, and actual crimes here. We don't have enough information here to investigate whether a crime has been committed. But we'll ask around and if we find anything, we'll be in touch. Do you have a number we can contact you on?"

Francesco wrote down his work number then gave his statement, his heart wrenching at the thought that Elena could be lying in a ditch somewhere or hurt in the street. What if it was too late? What if she was dead?

No, he refused to think that way. He had to be positive.

He brushed off those thoughts as he left the station. It was obvious the police would do nothing, so it was up to him. He was determined to find her, at whatever cost.

He walked the streets of Milan aimlessly in search of Elena, but she was nowhere in sight. Of course, he didn't expect her to pop up out of nowhere, but he had to start somewhere. She was missing, gone, lost, and the police thought she'd run away. It had to be the person harassing her. There was no other explanation for it. He should've done more to protect her. He should've kept her safe.

He flashed back to the times she'd told him about the snake her family confronted on their farm, and the time she was chastised for reading instead of doing chores. He knew all about her family, her friends, her secret ex-boyfriends, and the strict upbringing she'd experienced from her father. He knew about her sister Valeria, who had suffered at the hands of their father on more than one occasion. He felt for Elena's own growing independence and strong opinions because he had acted in the same way with his own father, who was strict too.

Coming out of his thoughts, Francesco ended up strolling along shopping strips of designer bargains along Corso Vittorio Emanuele II. He stared at the queue forming outside the shopping factory outlets. He looked inside, thinking that Elena might be searching for a bargain, and noticed how customers were crowded around clothing racks and elbowing their way through to other parts of the stores. He saw signs of discounts of up to 50 to70% off, given the end-of-season sales, and again, he wondered for an instant if Elena was in there snagging a bargain. As if she'd even be here. He was going mad.

Francesco continued walking along the outlet stores and ended up in the alternative and high street labels along Corso di Porta Ticinese with its smaller stores. Maybe this was where Elena would be. The chill in the air made him hug his body tight, and the fumes from the cars made him want to vomit. The congestion of crowds, the beeping of horns, and the unsteadiness of his feet on uneven, cracked concrete made him want to run away from this place. He was finally seeing a part of Milan he didn't like. The noise, pollution smells, and the hubbub of activity. Mostly, he enjoyed the stimulation, but not today. Not when he missed a beautiful woman so terribly.

Francesco's chest froze when he noticed the back of a woman with her smooth, long chestnut hair, her curvaceous and slim figure. Had he finally found Elena?

Francesco raced up ahead towards her and tapped her on the shoulder. The woman turned but instead of sporting Elena's warm eyes, these eyes were cold and grey. The woman pursed her lips and glared, jutting her dimpled chin.

He held up his hands in apology. "I'm sorry. I thought you were someone else."

The woman turned with a grunt. Francesco felt tears sting his eyes as he yearned for a different pair of eyes; Elena's eyes, her confident, vivacious nature, and her long healthy hair that gleamed in the sunlight. He was lost without her, and sat on a seat inside a door to lean his head into his hands. The tears fell easily.

CHAPTER 29
PURE MISERY

Elena came out of a deep slumber and rubbed her eyes. The putrid smell of sweat and discarded rubbish made her want to vomit. Her stomach felt rock hard and she soon realised she was holding her breath. There were bars all around her, and it took another few groggy minutes to understand that she was inside a human-sized cage. A deep weight pressed against her chest and a weakness fell over her legs and knees as she pushed hard against the bars. The sound of metal made her cringe with a hypersensitivity to noise she'd recently developed. Her skewed sense of time made her shudder. She didn't know if was daytime or night.

She also didn't know who had kidnapped her, but from her last memory, she'd been at the fashion show. She had drunk champagne that had made her dizzy and sick. She must've blacked out because the last thing she remembered was sitting in this cage but never seeing who had put her in here. Was it the person harassing her? It had to be.

A shiver of fear started deep in her stomach and spread.

If only the police had listened to her and helped investigate. Surely there were enough crimes where a person escalated to more serious crimes? Until then, the police weren't able to prosecute. They weren't even able to investigate, since terrorising someone wasn't considered a crime in the eyes of the law. It was ludicrous. How could this not be a crime when the trauma and fear of death was as bad as any other crime?

Elena massaged her legs and looked around her space carefully. She spotted a row of steel shelves filled with large boxes and a dust-filled tiled floor. A rubbish bin the size of a human body sat alongside the shelves. Other shelves with boxes sat behind her. It looked like some kind of warehouse, but it was abandoned. Maybe the boxes were empty or maybe they were archived documents.

Elena remembered feeling sick after the champagne, but she hadn't drunk much by that time. A waiter had given her the drink, but he hadn't offered anyone else drinks. She thought it was strange. Was the waiter her kidnapper? Had he put some kind of drug in her drink to incapacitate her? She'd been with Loredana, who had gone to the ladies' room. That window of time, after her friend had left but before she came back must've been when he had taken her. No one would think it was strange helping out a woman who was sick and possibly looking drunk. He would've pretended he was helping her when he was in fact kidnapping her. What other explanation could there be?

Her friends would be sick with worry. Even Nunziata and maybe Francesco. She wondered if Angelo was her kidnapper. He was angry enough with her to want to punish her for not having any interest in him. She didn't know anyone else who would do this to her, and she wondered if now the police would be searching for her. Surely someone would've gone to the police. They'd be here to find her by now.

Or maybe not. Maybe the person's plan was to starve her to death. She hadn't eaten anything since she'd awakened. She had woken up to a glass of water in her cage but that was it. Would he even feed her?

Elena leaned back against the cage, clearing her throat. Her water was finished but she was dry in the mouth again. She was famished, and her dress was torn and dirty at the hem. As she closed her eyes to shut out the pain, footsteps drew closer. She opened her eyes and shrank back at the approach of a hooded figure. The person who swaggered towards her wore a black hooded jacket, the brightest white sneakers, and a clown mask. His eyes gleamed with a cold light. He held a note in his left hand and a plate of sandwiches in the other. Slowly, he handed her a sandwich one at a time through the bars then pushed through the plate. Elena laid the sandwiches on the plate and quickly devoured the soft white bread. She tasted cheese, tomato, and lettuce. It was delicious. The man watched her eat, and Elena was too hungry to stop and talk. She bit into the other sandwich, then wiped her mouth with the back of her hand.

Turning to look at the man, she asked, "Why am I here, and what do you want from me?"

The man stared, saying nothing. He unfolded the note and pushed it through the bars. Elena grabbed the note and read it. It said, *"If you want your life back, you need to leave Milan and return to your hometown of Laurino. If you don't leave, then I will have no choice but to make trouble for your friends and hurt whoever else is close to you. Agree to leave Milan and I will release you soon."*

Elena swallowed, her head feeling heavy all of a sudden. She lifted her head up and watched him. "Why do you want me to leave? I'm studying." She angled her head. "I'm not hurting anyone here." The man shook his head but said nothing. "Please. Tell me what I've done to you. This doesn't make sense. I need answers." Again, he stared but said nothing. A minute later, he rose. "No, please don't go. Tell me why I should leave. I deserve some kind of explanation. Please!"

As the man was walking away, Elena screamed, "Angelo, you'll pay for this. You won't get away with this."

He didn't answer. Tears scalded her cheeks as silence surrounded her again. Darkness fell upon her.

Some time later, Elena thought about the man who'd been here. She suddenly wasn't sure her kidnapper was Angelo. The man in the clown mask seemed taller and older, like someone she didn't know. Was he going to release her or was that a trick to let her guard down for whatever warped reason he had? She had to have hope that she would be released. Otherwise she wouldn't get through this.

CHAPTER 30
BROKEN PROMISE

The next morning, Elena extended her legs against the cage and pushed with all her might. She kicked the door with its padlocked key, but it wouldn't budge. Several more kicks left her puffing. It was no use. She couldn't get out of the cage. It was too tightly locked.

She rubbed the side of her neck, feeling the cricks, and exhaled. Her whole body was stiff, and a migraine pressed hard against her eyes and head. She was helpless and weak and would never get out of here. This man would probably keep her here to die, possibly feeding her less and less every day. Heavy footsteps sounded on the floor, and the man came in wearing a long coat, a wide-brimmed hat, and the clown mask. This time he sat on the ground and stared. Out of one pocket, he took a plastic-wrapped sandwich and handed it to her through the bars. From his other pocket, he took a piece of paper and shoved another small note into her cage. Again, she read the note. *"As you tried to escape just now, I think I'll keep you a little while longer. Who knows! Maybe forever. It seems as though you're not taking me seriously. You need to learn your lesson."*

Elena shook her head. "No, please don't do this. I promise I'll be good. Please let me go. I've leave Milan if you want me to, but don't keep me in here. I'm in so much pain. Please, whoever you are. I know you're not a bad person."

The man laughed and threw his head back. He placed his hands on the ground and pushed to his feet. He watched her for a minute, then walked out without a sound.

"No! Let me go! Help me. Don't do this!"

Elena drew her hands through her sweaty scalp. He didn't bring water this time. He was slowly killing her. Next time, he probably wouldn't even bring her food. She wondered how long he planned to keep her in this cage. She had to get out. She couldn't wait here to die as she didn't deserve this torture. She'd never hurt anyone in her life.

A glint of metal on the floor of her cage caught her eye. A bobby pin. It must've fallen out of her hair when she swept her hand through it. Maybe that was her ticket out. She'd never picked a lock before, but there was no harm in trying. Maybe the pin would get her out. She pondered for a moment, wondering how the man knew she had tried to escape. There had to be cameras in here. He must've been watching her every move. She'd have to be careful.

Elena could always wait until night-time when he'd most likely be asleep, but there were bound to be times during the day that would be safe for an attempt. After all, he couldn't be watching her all day. He had to have a job—unless he was in Milan temporarily. Maybe he wasn't even Italian.

There was so much she didn't know.

Elena waited a moment. There was no time like the present. If he did see her, she would hit him with her shoes. She slipped them off and glanced around. Somehow, she had to get out of here. The bobby pin was her chance. Maybe it wouldn't work but she'd give it all her strength and focus.

Looking around to make sure the man didn't return, she grabbed the pin, put her hands through the bar, and cradled her hand around the lock with the pin held between her thumb and index finger. Swiftly, Elena pushed the pin into the slot of the padlock, but nothing budged. She brought the pin back into the cage and waited a moment to see if he would come rushing in. If he did, then she'd know he'd been watching her.

Ten minutes passed and no one came. She tried again to pick the lock. Again, nothing opened. Again and again, the sweat popping out on her forehead. She sighed and shook her head and slammed her hand against the cage. "Dammit! This has to work. There has to be some way to jimmy this damn lock."

She waited and closed her eyes, getting her body and mind relaxed. Then she tried again. Carefully, she placed the pin into the slot of the padlock and turned it gently in a variety of directions. This had to work. Her life depended on it.

Elena was determined to get out of here. Again, she tried the lock. Then again, and again. With a calm breath, she stayed focused and believed in the lock. She became the lock and kept going with ease. There was no point in getting worked up about it. Anything she did had to be done with a relaxed and calm mind. She could do this.

Just before as she was about to give it a rest, the padlock opened. She smiled to herself and unlocked the cage. In a rapid action, she scurried out of the cage, grabbed her shoes and pin, then ran out as if her life depended on it. The place was like a maze, but eventually, she found a door.

It was locked. Damn! He had locked the door from outside.

Elena scanned the warehouse. The boxes. Maybe there was something inside one of them. There had to be something in here that would slam open the door.

Quickly she opened box after box. All empty. She tried a row of boxes, then ran to the other side of the warehouse, her bare feet slapping on the concrete floor. Still nothing. She was staring into another empty box when a thought came. Her pin! She could try to jimmy the lock to the outer door with her pin.

She closed the box and edged to the outside door, listening closely for the man's return. Then, placing the pin into the slot, she tried to remember how the pin was directed when it opened the cage. She closed her eyes, became the lock, and it came to her. The exact direction of the pin. Voila! She heard a clicking noise. Swinging open the handle, the door unlocked, and she breathed in the mild, sunlit air. The beginning of spring was here, she realised. The weather gave her a sigh of relief.

Quickly, she glanced around. The street was empty, but who knew how long that would last?

Elena ran. Twigs and pebbles bit into her feet, but she plunged on.

There was nothing around the area, so she let her feet move quicker than her confused mind. Running and running, through fields and towering trees. She stopped to put on her shoes for protection from boulders, stones, and rocks. The smell of smoke was prominent and houses in the distance kept her going. She might not have much time before the man had a chance to look at the camera.

CHAPTER 31
AN ILLUSION OF FUTILITY

Francesco sighed as he steered onto Elena's street. Loredana sat in the passenger seat and Isabella settled behind Loredana in the back seat. They both looked stricken, their eyes black and weepy from missing Elena. Francesco hadn't slept in the past two days, since Elena went missing, and now he wanted to make sure she hadn't returned home without telling them. He had spoken to Angelo but that was a dead end.

Isabella broke into his thoughts. "You know I honestly thought that Angelo might've done something to Elena."

Francesco wanted to wring the guy's neck for harassing Elena in and outside of class. "As much as I hate the guy, I honestly think he was telling the truth. He didn't seem to know where she was. Besides, I don't think he's smart enough to pull this off if she was kidnapped."

Loredana tilted her head as he turned off the engine. "What do you mean, if she was kidnapped? What else could this be? You of all people should realise that she wouldn't leave without saying goodbye. I thought you understood her."

Francesco sat quietly in the driver's seat, bowing his head. "I do understand her, and I—oh never mind!"

Loredana looked at him strangely. "What were you about to say Francesco? Huh?"

He opened his door. "Nothing. Let's go!"

Isabella and Loredana exited the car, then walked up the path to the house. Nunziata opened the door before they knocked. She swung it open and let them inside, leading them to the kitchen area. They sat around looking at each other, and Nunziata frowned.

"Nothing yet?"

Francesco turned to her. "We thought she might've come back. We had to see for ourselves."

"I would've called you, Francesco. Don't you trust me?" Nunziata said. The words were right, but the chill in her voice told him things were still far from well between them.

Maybe it was time to make amends. If he could. "Look, Nunziata," he said. "I am so sorry about Domenico. But he made

99

his own choices, and he didn't die by my hands. I know that sounds horrible, but it's the truth."

Nunziata stood up, frozen in her spot. Her jaw clenched, and she seemed about to fly into him when Loredana intervened. "Nunziata. Whatever you and Francesco have going on, we don't have time for that. We have to work together on this situation. Have you called her family?"

Nunziata stared at Francesco for what seemed like minutes. Then she looked away and let out a long breath. "No. I was hoping we'd find her before I had to do that. Why worry them if we don't have to?"

Isabella clasped her hands together. "I'm worried about her, but the police haven't told us anything. I wonder if they're even looking for her."

Nunziata grunted. "Of course not! They're too busy helping the politicians, the corrupt, and the wealthy to worry about a poor twenty-year-old who could be lying in a ditch somewhere. God forbid they ever did some real work."

"Please, Nunziata," Francesco said. "Stop it! She's fine. I have to believe that. She can't be hurt. She just can't."

Nunziata pursed her lips and let out an audible breath. "You act like you care about her, but I know what you're like with the girls. She's merely another notch on your belt. The way you used to gallivant with a different woman every night in the village. It was disgusting. Elena is innocent and doesn't deserve to be with a womaniser like you."

Loredana held up her hand. "Please stop this. It's not helping."

Francesco ignored her. "I was young and naive then. I've grown up a lot since that time. I truly care about Elena and would never hurt her."

Nunziata watched him carefully, as if a thought crossed her mind. "There's something you're hiding, isn't there? Something you don't want anyone to know. What is it?"

Francesco felt nauseous. He had to be strong and hide what he was truly feeling. "Nothing, okay? I'm just worried about Elena. We have to think about what to do next. Maybe we could go to the police and put more pressure on them. Or maybe we could put an advertisement in the paper. Someone might've seen her around."

"And you're dreaming," Loredana said. "If she was kidnapped, then this was done discreetly."

Francesco turned to her. "Are you sure there wasn't anyone around you guys that night? Maybe someone you forgot about."

Loredana shrugged. "No one, really. Only the waiter!" Her eyes widened. "The waiter. He only served us that night. I grabbed a glass of champagne from him and so did Elena. After that she became quiet, but I thought she was tired, so I went to the bathroom and thought nothing of it. I wasn't gone for long. Then she disappeared."

Isabella angled her head. "It might've been the waiter. Is there anyone we can ask about who worked that night?"

Loredana said, "Elena knew some of the organisers, but I don't know anyone."

Francesco rose and rubbed his hands in excitement. "The institute would know who we can contact. If someone wasn't meant to be serving drinks that night, then it had to be orchestrated by the waiter. Let's go and ask!"

As Loredana and Isabella rose from their seats, footsteps sounded behind them. Francesco turned around. He lost all coherent thought. Elena! His beloved Elena.

She managed a smile on weary feet then collapsed on the kitchen floor in front of them.

CHAPTER 32
RECOUNTING EVENTS

Elena opened her eyes, feeling a soft cloth dabbing her cheeks. She lay on the couch and felt like her body was about to collapse. Francesco was wiping her face, his eyes dark and stern.

Loredana was staring at her from a nearby chair, while Isabella sat with her head bowed. Was she crying?

Nunziata walked in and laid an extra pillow under her head, a reassuring smile plastered across her face. She knit her brows, then stood over Francesco, eventually grabbing the cloth from his hands and resuming his action. Francesco shook his head but said nothing as he stood behind Nunziata with his arms crossed. He sighed and turned away, then sat on an armchair beside the couch. Nunziata stopped wiping Elena's face and drew a hand over her fringe. Elena had never thought her landlady would be this nurturing, almost mother-like. She must've missed her terribly.

Her legs, back, and head throbbed and ached. Her vision was a little blurred from her headache. She pressed hard into her temples as she slowly lifted herself up into a sitting position on the couch. Her eyes roamed around the living area and her loved ones, her chest feeling heavy with pain and ongoing fear. She'd never thought she'd get out of that cage alive, even though her captor had fed her and said he had planned to let her go. He hadn't been cruel, at least not yet, but that didn't excuse him for kidnapping her.

Nunziata turned to the others who waited for Elena to speak. "Can you tell us what happened, Elena? We were all sick with worry."

Francesco approached Elena and knelt in front of her. As she sank back against the couch, he took hold of her hand. Where did she begin?

The look on Nunziata's face turned serious. "How are you feeling?"

Elena tilted her head. "Pretty sore everywhere. I need a shower."

Loredana held back her tears. "Oh, gorgeous, you were gone for two days. Of course you need a shower."

Isabella turned to Elena. "I'm glad you're okay, but shouldn't we be calling the police? They'll need her statement."

Nunziata gestured with her hand as if dismissing her. "She can do that later. Right now, we need to know what happened to her."

Elena clasped her hands, rubbing into her knuckles. She took a calming breath and started recounting her nightmare. They listened without interruption, and she wondered whether any of them had a clue as to who would do this to her. It had to be the person terrorising her. There was no other explanation.

"What I don't understand is why he wants me to leave Milan. I mean, this is my future we're talking about." She cleared her throat. "He even threatened to hurt my family and friends if I don't leave, so what choice do I have?"

Francesco kissed the back of Elena's hand. "No, you're not listening to some madman. We'll find whoever did this and bring him to justice. There's no way you're leaving. We'll be fine"

Elena shook her head. "But I can't risk you guys getting hurt. I have to go home, Francesco. It's the only way." She ached for him as his eyes fixed on hers. Oh, how she cared deeply for this man, but could they ever be together? Something was holding him back.

Loredana intervened. "Listen, you give your statement to the police and they'll protect you. Don't worry about us. We're fighters. Besides, it sounds like he has some humanity, so I doubt he'd attempt to kill us. He just said that to scare you, that's all. But we'll still be vigilant and careful, and make sure we're always with someone until the police find this guy."

Nunziata chuckled. "We're talking about the Milan police here, Loredana. We have a greater chance of getting an earthquake than the police catching this man. This won't be a priority case for them. Not only that, but they don't care about their people. Never did and never will."

"All the more reason I need to leave," said Elena.

Nunziata pursed her lips. "You will do no such thing. So long as you travel with someone else, this bastard won't come after you. He sounds weak."

Elena had a thought. "The strange thing was that he never spoke to me. He only communicated in letters."

Isabella perked up. "Do you think it's someone you might know? That maybe he thought you would've recognised his voice?"

Elena nodded. "No doubt. It could be Angelo."

Isabella shrugged. "I don't know, Elena. Would he resort to kidnapping? I mean, I know he likes you, but I don't think that's his style."

Francesco leaned in. "I think she's right. He's not that clever."

Elena wasn't sure about anything anymore, except for her feelings towards Francesco. She was frightened that her kidnapper would escalate, especially now that she had escaped.

CHAPTER 33
CONFRONTATION

Elena gave her statement to the police first thing the next morning and they promised they'd investigate. However, neither she nor Francesco expected much from them. It was a good thing she'd relied on herself to escape her kidnapper.

She scurried out of the station with Isabella who, at Francesco's request, had stayed over at her place last night. This was going to be a nightmare if she needed babysitting everywhere she went. Elena was twenty years old, and in spite of being kidnapped, she could take care of herself. Maybe her kidnapper had given up on her by now. Or maybe he wasn't even in the country anymore.

Elena and Isabella hopped on a bus and sat towards the front. She'd missed a couple of days of classes and hoped she'd be able to catch up on the work she'd missed.

It was crowded at the back of the bus, and she stared into some of the eyes of the men, pondering whether any of them was her kidnapper. Was she passing by him without even knowing he was still watching her? Would he try to hurt her again?

A tug on her shoulder alerted her towards her friend.

"I said, are you looking forward to school?"

Elena nodded. "Does the institute know what happened to me?"

Isabella nodded. "Valentina said that the police had contacted the co-ordinator to ask questions and explain what had happened to you. They were pretty sympathetic and will want to ask you questions."

"What kinds of questions?"

Isabella shrugged. "Well, I guess they were trying to figure out if anyone else was missing from the school the last couple of days. Maybe see whether anyone you knew took you." Isabella stared. "Angelo was at school while you were missing, so I don't think it was him."

"I don't even know what time it was when the man came to me, but it could've been night-time, Isabella. I'd lost all track of time, so Angelo could've come here, then visited me in the night."

Elena looked beyond the buildings, cafes, and restaurants and noticed storm clouds brewing. Billowing trees unnerved her, and trickles of water fell as people rushed to and fro to take cover under sheltered shops or awnings.

The bus passed the small shops that housed vintage clothing, street wear, and original accessories lined along Corso di Porta Ticinese. She missed browsing in those stores, even though she'd been gone for only two days. It felt like she'd been out of action for two weeks, and now she was unsure of who she could trust. She hadn't made any enemies, but she obviously had one.

***

Valentina waltzed into the room and headed straight to Elena, who was sitting beside Isabella. Angelo sat on her other side, and while Elena ignored him, she could see from the corner of her eye that he was staring at her.

"Darling, are you okay? I heard what happened."

"I'm fine, Valentina. Thanks for asking."

Valentina drew her bejewelled wrist through her hair. "Well, if there's anything you need, please let me know." She moved towards the front, took notes and documents out of her bag, and cleared her throat. "Now everyone, may I have your attention?" She waited for a few late-comers to arrive and gave them a stern expression of warning.

Elena turned towards Angelo and felt sick to the stomach. As he watched her, he licked his lips with a sneer. Why was he giving her that look? It had to be him showing her he had the upper hand. She turned away and focused her attention on the teacher.

Valentina went on. "Now today, we'll be looking at creating a fashion portfolio and a collection of diverse fashion. This is the beginning of your new careers, people. Your illustrious careers, so make sure you give yourselves enough time to get a start on this as it will inform your final marks for this year. We're already halfway through so you'll need to get your heads down without any distractions. None at all. You will live, breathe, and sleep fashion. Sleep is overrated at this time, people. You are on your way to creating your own brand of fashion, your speciality that will mark you in the fashion world. Now, are there any questions before we begin?"

A show of hands came up, and Elena blocked out the questions when Angelo whispered, "So, where were you the last couple of days? I missed you."

"I think you know where I was."

Angelo knit his brows. "At home lazing around."

Elena lowered her voice and said fiercely, "You kidnapped me, didn't you? Kept me locked up like an animal in that cage."

Angelo's eyes widened, his body drawing back as if he'd been struck by a bullet. "What the hell are you talking about? You were kidnapped?"

He was either a great actor or he genuinely didn't know what had happened to her. She tested him further. "It was you, wasn't it? You can't get a girl to go out with you, so you kidnap them instead. Real smooth, Angelo. Real smooth."

His hands clenched and his cheeks blushed. "You stupid bitch! How the hell dare you say such a ludicrous thing?"

Valentina looked at them and held up a hand. "What is going on here, Angelo? I will not tolerate abusive language in my classroom."

Angelo bowed his head, his face flushed. Elena looked at Isabella, who patted her on the shoulder. "Sorry, Miss," Elena said.

"I want you both outside. Now!"

Valentina, Angelo, and Elena both exited the classroom as stunned faces stared after them. They stood outside the door with Angelo shuffling his feet and avoiding their eyes while Elena watched him cower next to her.

"Now, why did you call Elena a bitch? Do you even know what she's been through?"

Angelo took his hands out of his pockets and swallowed. "Miss, she told me about being kidnapped or something, and accused me. I mean, I've been in class the whole time. I'm not the psycho that she thinks I am."

She turned to Elena. "Is that true?"

Elena shrugged. "I might've, but only because he's been giving me a hard time in class. Just because I wouldn't go out with him. I thought that maybe he was trying to get back at me."

Valentina scrunched up her nose as if contemplating the thought. "And is there any evidence to suggest that Angelo was your kidnapper? Has the police found something?"

"Well no, but I thought it was him."

Valentina grabbed Angelo by the shoulders. "Tell me the truth, Angelo. Did you have anything to do with the kidnapping of Elena or know of anyone who might?"

He gave a strangled little laugh. "Oh, this is ridiculous. I could never hurt anyone like that. You have to believe me."

"I believe you, but I will not tolerate name-calling in my classroom. Do you understand, Angelo?"

He stared down at his feet. "Yes, Miss."

"And you, Elena. That's a huge thing to accuse someone of without evidence. I expect you to keep quiet in class when others are asking questions, as both of you could learn something. Now let's get inside."

Elena followed Valentina inside the room and felt the muffled sigh from Angelo behind her. She remembered thinking her abductor seemed older than her classmate. *Could Angelo actually be innocent?*

CHAPTER 34
ESCALATED ANGER

The man pulled down his hood, watching from a distance while Elena stepped into her residence with her friend Isabella. She was taking extreme measures to make sure she didn't go anywhere alone. That would make things trickier. How would he get her back now and teach her a very important lesson? He had to find another way, and he was not about to give up.

He couldn't believe the bitch had escaped, even after he stressed how he'd let her leave. She couldn't wait to get back to her cushy life with her pompous attitude. Elena thought she was better and smarter than him, but she didn't know how smart he could be. She didn't know what he could be capable of. Boy, would she be in for a surprise.

How dare she make him look weak by escaping? Now she'd gone and made things worse because he was doubly-mad. She wasn't going to get away next time. He'd make sure she would no longer be laughing with her friends or family. She would either leave Milan or he would hurt her so badly that she wouldn't be able to live comfortably again. He'd wipe that smart attitude off her face, and then she'd know who was the winner. He wouldn't be made a fool of again. Never again!

He didn't have any plan as yet, but he had plenty of time to concoct one. First of all, he'd lie low. Long enough for her to start feeling comfortable and relaxed, then bam! He would get her again when she least expected it. He was great with disguises, so he could be anyone he wanted to be.

She was beautiful, he had to admit. Although not enough to stop his plan from brewing. She would not get away with staying in Milan. He wanted her to leave and she had no right to stay. This wasn't her rightful place. Her place was in the village where she could find a nice Italian man to marry. Her job was to cook and clean for a husband whose whims she could cater to. Her place was not in Milan. Milan was his territory.

CHAPTER 35
SHARING WITH FRIENDS

Almost a month later in March, Elena felt like she could have a night out. She was certain her kidnapper had moved on as she hadn't heard a peep from him. Everything was back to normal, and she was having a night out with Loredana, Isabella, and Francesco. Even Loredana's boyfriend was joining them.

Elena was walking in Navigli near the canals of Milan, with Isabella, the reflection of all the small pubs and ancient trattorias shining in the surface of the water. Crowds flocked around the pubs and restaurants, with a footbridge over the water creating an even more spectacular view. They headed around the columns of San Lorenzo in the area of Porta Ticinese along Via Torino until eventually reaching Piazza Duomo. Elena hugged her body tight as her jacket failed to keep her warm in the windy, chilled night.

The smells of spilled beer and spicy food filled the air, mixed with a range of perfumes and colognes amidst the crowd. Elena stared at the gathering of people sitting on the ground, sharing drinks and snacks around the columns. She turned to Isabella, who was searching for their friends.

"So, what is this place?" Elena said. "It looks amazing." She turned to face the many bars surrounding the San Lorenzo ruin.

Isabella smiled and touched her on the shoulder. "This is what's known as the place for the penniless because they offer drinks very cheaply at these bars. It gets busy, so I don't know if the others are here yet. We might not find a place to sit."

Elena's teeth were chattering as she roamed the area, but she couldn't find Francesco and Loredana. She needed a drink to warm up, but that might not be happening any time soon if they couldn't find their friends.

People sitting on the ground chattered, laughed, and seemed to be engrossed in their own group, but she felt she was being watched. It was crazy. She couldn't see anyone, but a tremble moved up and down her spine and she couldn't shake it off. The crowd unnerved her, and the noise was almost unbearable. Once she shared a drink with her friends, she'd be more relaxed.

Her kidnapper was surely not around any longer. He must've grown tired of her. She was just being paranoid after what she'd been through.

"Elena, Isabella, over here," said a disembodied voice from the distance.

Elena searched for the voice, finally spotting Francesco waving them over about twenty metres ahead. He sat in a huddle with Loredana and Biagio.

They scurried over and greeted their friends with an embrace, but both shaking Biagio's hand.

Elena and Isabella sat around the huddle. A can of some kind of sparkling drink was pushed into her hand. She opened it and drank it down as if it was heaven. Quickly, it warmed her up and her teeth stopped chattering.

Francesco watched Elena. "I'm so glad you came. It's been a while since you've been out."

Loredana nodded. "Great to see you, girl. Biagio here has even missed you."

Biagio smiled and held Loredana's hand. "She's right. We haven't been out since that restaurant. How have you been?"

Elena's throat felt dry. Had Loredana told him what had happened? Her cheeks felt flushed, but she ignored it. "Never better. I just love this place. It's buzzing with excitement."

Isabella gave her a reassuring smile. "Next up, we're hitting one of the nightclubs. Are you okay with that?"

Elena hesitated. "Sure thing."

Elena noticed Francesco's eyes lingering on her. He turned away when she spotted him staring. Her chest felt warm and fuzzy, and her body yearned for his. She could barely think or breathe while they drank over small talk and laughs. She could barely find enough words to string a sentence together. A magnet drew her to Francesco, especially when his shoulder brushed hers as he reached for another drink.

They all rose and headed towards Francesco's car. He drove them to a nightclub and parked his car a short walk away. Once they entered the club, Elena came across a swarm of beautiful women wearing dresses that barely matched the winter season, their cleavage and bare flesh exposed for all to see. The men wore trendy winter attire and kept themselves rugged up in the dark ambience of the nightclub with its beating rhythms that pounded in her head. She wasn't ready for all these people pressing up against her as they walked through the crowd to search for a table.

When finally sitting at an empty table, Elena turned to see a man staring at her. He winked and blew her a kiss. She felt her heart beating fast and her mind racing. Was this her kidnapper, and was he taunting her? Now she was definitely being paranoid.

CHAPTER 36
A HOT STEAMY NIGHT

Loud music, cigarette smoke, and sweat surrounded her as Elena pushed and navigated her way through the flocking crowds in the nightclub. Disco balls and lights hung from the ceiling and a stage up ahead displayed a disc jockey steering a turntable while his head shook like a flying mosquito. Parts of the crowd moved in rhythm to the music while others held drinks or sat by tables in the least crowded corners of the room. Bartenders served a few people from the bar, but when a few patrons moved towards the dance floor, they held a glass in one hand and a cigarette or cigar in the other. How could they drink and smoke at the same time, Elena thought, let alone dance? Why even smoke at all? She couldn't tolerate the burning fumes that caused her to cough and made her eyes water.

Elena felt warm hands on the small of her back. She turned to see Francesco move her along towards an empty table, his gaze roaming as if he was looking for someone.

"Are you okay?" Elena shouted among the chatter and noise.

He nodded. "Just some of these guys keep gawking at you so I'm making sure they keep their hands to themselves."

Elena smiled to herself. "And would that be such a bad thing? A guy noticing me?"

Francesco looked away and shrugged.

Loredana interrupted their moment. "Listen guys. We're going to dance. Isabella's coming with us, so you guys get to be on your own." She winked at Elena, who could've killed her for saying such a thing.

Francesco drew in a long breath and gazed at Elena. Her face warmed and her hands shook, so she placed them underneath the table. His lingering stare unnerved her, but it also caused her adrenaline to spike. The music blared as their friends scurried into the middle of the dance floor and squeezed themselves through a small space. Biagio smiled at both Loredana and Isabella, obviously attempting to make Isabella feel welcome among them.

Several men walked past and gaped at Elena. One of them stopped and approached. He wore a tight-fitted t-shirt and sported stubble with dishevelled hair.

"Would you like to dance?"

Elena looked over at Francesco. His eyes were narrowed and his hands turned into fists. Was he about to explode? She wanted to say yes to make him jealous, but that would be childish. Besides, she wasn't sure she could trust anyone after her kidnapping experience. She couldn't be sure the man wasn't still hanging around, but she doubted it. He had most likely moved on.

"No thanks."

The man gestured with his hands. "Oh, come on. The dance floor is just over there, and you're too gorgeous not to have a man by your side."

Elena smiled. "No thank you. I'm good."

The man feigned a cry, his feet stuck by her side. He wasn't about to budge anytime soon.

Francesco approached. "Listen, she's my girlfriend, so get lost."

The man suddenly drew back. He held up his hands, saying, "Sorry, man," and walked off.

Elena felt a flutter at the comment. She watched Francesco as he grabbed her by the hand. "Let's dance."

She was led by his gentle prod until they reached a quieter part of the dance floor and both swayed to the music. His stares caused her heart to flutter and her body to burn like fire. He moved closer and laid his hands around her waist, moving in rhythm to her body. Then when a slow ballad played, Francesco wrapped his arms tighter around her body and drew her close, his hands caressing the small of her back. Elena got lost in the music and felt his gentle yet manly hands explore her upper spine and travel back down to her hips. His aftershave was strong with a musky scent, and his breathing was heavy.

The music stopped, and Francesco said, "Let's get out of here."

Elena didn't question him when he led her out of the nightclub and towards a nearby park. His hand feathered her cheeks as he gently pushed her against the trunk of a tree. His lips parted as he pressed himself against her, his lips crushing hers.

Elena felt his tongue probing her mouth, the warmth arousing her as she kissed him back and moaned in response.

He pulled away for a moment and gazed. "I care about you so much, Elena. So much it hurts."

Elena's vocal cords felt so tight she couldn't speak. Instead, her eyes told him how much she wanted him, so he streamed kisses around her neck and throat and drew his hands through her hair. Then his hands lingered over her breasts, teasing her nipples until they stood erect. She opened up further to his hot French kiss, and yearned for more. She wanted him to be her first experience. She wanted to feel him deeply inside her.

His hands moved down to her hips, then down to the edge of her underwear. He started to push them down until a rustle of leaves sounded nearby. Both of them stopped and turned but couldn't see anyone.

Francesco turned to Elena and gave her a quick kiss. "I think we should go."

"You're right. This is a public place."

Francesco stroked her cheek. "You are so beautiful, Elena, and I want you so badly, but not this way. It has to be special."

Elena nodded. "What did you have in mind?"

"My place. Just you and me tonight."

Elena swallowed. "And what about the others?"

"We'll make our excuses and I'll drop them off home."

"Okay. Your place it is."

Francesco walked back with her towards the nightclub, his arm lingering around her waist. "What about Nunziata? Will she be waiting up for you?"

"Don't worry about her. She doesn't wait up, but I can tell her I spent the night at Isabella's place."

"Cheeky girl!" He gave her a wink, and together they forged ahead.

Elena's nerves tingled, but then an intervening thought disturbed her. That rustling in the leaves... What if someone had been watching them?

CHAPTER 37
MIXED EMOTIONS

Later that night, Elena walked into Francesco's house, her voice suddenly disappearing. She felt her body shake and wondered if she was rushing into this. Yet she cared about Francesco deeply and knew this was the right thing to do. The only thing stopping her was the thought that her kidnapper might've been watching them in the park. She hadn't heard from him for a while, so surely, she was secure. Francesco made her feel safe and loved, and she trusted him completely. They were great friends with a strong connection, and had liked each other for months so she hoped she was ready to do this and wouldn't pull out at the last minute.

He set her down at the kitchen table and she spotted the spick and span bench space and empty dishes in the sink. "Would you like a drink?"

"No thanks." Her voice sounded shaky.

Francesco sat beside her. "Are you sure about this? You seem nervous."

Elena clasped her hands. "It's my first time, Francesco. I'm a virgin." Francesco's face flushed and he turned away. His eyes turned serious but he said nothing. "Francesco. Are you okay?"

He looked at her and linked his fingers around her palm. "If I knew that, I'd never have rushed you into this. I'm sorry. I never thought you were a virgin. I mean, you're so beautiful. I thought maybe there'd been someone serious before me."

Elena smiled. "There were a couple of boyfriends back in Laurino, but with my papa around, I could never do much more than kiss. He would've killed me."

"And now wouldn't he hate what we're about to do?"

"I'm an adult and don't live under his roof. I'm my own person. My poor sister suffered because of his temper, but he has mellowed a little after all these years."

Francesco rose and poured himself a glass of water. He turned to Elena and pulled her up from the seat. Gently he led her to his bedroom that featured posters of fashion week, fashion awards, and framed pictures of a beautiful woman.

"Who is she?"

Francesco glanced fondly at the nearest picture. "My mother when she was young."

"She was beautiful."

"And still is. Exactly like you."

Francesco faltered. He lapsed into silence but didn't move. Was he pondering something, or was he having second thoughts?

"What's going on, Francesco?"

He shook his head, as if pulling himself back to the present. "I'm taking you home. This isn't right. It's too soon, and you're a virgin. I can't take advantage of you like this. Not when—"

Elena tilted her head. "When what?" She held on to his hands, but he pushed her away.

"Nothing. I'll take you home."

Elena's chest deflated. She wanted nothing more than to be held by Francesco and to be loved by him. He was worried just because she was a virgin, but she didn't think there'd be anyone else in her life but him. He was truly special.

Elena grabbed him by the hands. She pressed them against her lips, her throat, and her breasts. "Love me, Francesco. Love me completely. This is so right."

She could feel him warring with his own desires. Then in a sudden burst of energy, Francesco gently pushed her down on the bed and kissed her hungrily. He unzipped and pulled off her dress and threw it across the floor, then explored her body with caressing hands. His lips trailed down the outline of her bra, her belly, and legs until he unclipped her bra and caressed her small breasts. He kissed both her nipples and caressed her stomach, then kissed her again fully on the lips.

All of a sudden, he moved off her body and picked up her dress. He shook his head. "This doesn't feel right. I can't take advantage of you this way. At least not tonight."

Elena grabbed the dress from his shaky hands and slipped it on. She fought back the tears. "But I told you I was ready. Why did you stop?"

He looked up at the ceiling as if he couldn't face her. Drawing his hands through his hair, he softly said, "I think we need to have a few more dates and see how we feel then. I'd like to get to know you more, and I'm sure we can spare a few days out together. I mean, you're a virgin and that's precious."

"You say that as if you're not totally committed to me. Is this just going to be a fling for you? Is that all I am to you?"

Francesco sighed and sat himself down at the edge of the bed. He stared straight into her eyes, looking disappointed. "I can't believe you even think that about me. You are the real deal for me, and I care about you so much it hurts. Please believe that."

He sounded so authentic and genuine that she believed him. Maybe she was letting her physical arousal guide her into rushing headlong into a sexual relationship. She didn't even know what to expect, even though she had come close in the past.

After they both dressed, Francesco swallowed. Then grabbing her hand, he led her outside his house and towards the car.

CHAPTER 38
A NEW RELATIONSHIP

Elena sank her feet into the lush green lawn as crowds journeyed along the jogging tracks around a transparent lake. Francesco walked alongside her, gazing into her eyes as he spoke.

"The Sempione Park is one of the largest parks in Milan. There's the Milan City Aquarium, an art exhibition tower, a Japanese garden, and a public library." He pointed at a distance. "At the entrance, which I forgot to mention earlier is the Arco della Pace."

Elena nodded. "What is the Arco della Pace?"

Francesco set out a thick blanket on the green lawn then placed a large picnic basket onto it. "Well, obviously about peace, but particularly about the celebration of Napoleon's victories. It's pretty popular with the more modern architects, and around the monument you've got heaps of bars, clubs, and restaurants for the locals and tourists."

"It's certainly something I'll never forget. It's beautiful."

Francesco took her hand and kissed the back of it. "And you're beautiful too." He winked, then reached over and kissed her gently on the lips. Elena found herself blushing as she remembered their intimacy a week ago. In the last week, Francesco had taken her to restaurants and the movies almost every night. They had got to know each other on an emotional level and had bonded more intensely.

Elena brushed aside her thoughts. She drank in the sunshine warming her cheeks and the fresh fern smells of bushy trees that billowed in the light wind. The mild breeze brushed against her cheeks, as she relished the month of March; the beginning of spring. She sat on the blanket and watched passers-by who were either couples walking hand in hand, children running around the lake and feeding birds, or joggers running around the tracks dodging people. The noise surrounding them was calming because of the elation associated with the sounds.

Francesco dug into the picnic basket and brought out a container of prosciutto, fresh rolls of ciabatta, assorted cheeses, salami, and panettone for dessert.

Elena and Francesco made themselves a roll. "Are you feeding an army here?"

Francesco shrugged as he filled his roll with the ingredients and bit into it. He wiped his mouth with the back of his hand, a crumb remaining on his bottom lip. Elena wiped it away as Francesco took hold of her hand and fixed his gaze on her.

He set down his roll. "I just wanted to ask you a question."

Elena nodded. "Sure."

"About last week. Are you glad we didn't rush into things?"

Elena swallowed. She couldn't lie. "I can't say I wasn't disappointed, but I understand your need to wait. Maybe I was thinking with my body rather than my head that night."

Francesco's eyes bored into her. "I cannot wait to be intimate with you, but only when you're completely ready and not earlier than that. It is Sunday today, so I'm all yours."

Elena looked away, as if his eyes burned sensually into her skin. Her heart raced, and her throat felt parched. She grabbed a bottle of water from the basket and drank it down. She wondered if there was a double-meaning in his last comment about being his all day today. She felt a trickle of sweat down her back and yet oddly aroused.

"Are you okay?" He asked.

"Hmmm. I'm just still a bit nervous about all this. It's all new to me."

"And I'm here to tell you that we'll go at your pace."

Elena said her piece. "And what if I am ready?"

His eyes lit up. "Really? Are you sure about that?"

Elena nodded.

"Well maybe before we get into that, I'd like to give you something." He reached into the basket for a heart-shaped box and handed it to her.

Elena cocked her head. "What's this?"

"A little something to honour the beginning of our relationship. Something to remember me by when I'm not with you."

Elena drew a quick breath and slowly flipped open the box. Her hands shook as she took out a gold bracelet with her name engraved on it. Several heart charms hung on the bracelet. It was exquisite. "I love it, but this is too much."

He shook his head. "Only the best for someone I adore. I'll put it on for you." He guided his hand around the jewellery and clicked it into place around her wrist. Elena felt truly spoiled and loved. She'd wear it every day.

Elena and Francesco enjoyed the silence as they savoured their rolls, watching the birds flock around them. Citrus smells filled the air as if the birds bathed in it. She turned her eyes to the distance, and a looming figure flashed before her. A large man was dressed in a hooded coat, wearing dark glasses and loose-fitting pants. He watched her for a moment. Then he disappeared towards the exit of the park behind trees. *What the hell!*

***

Elena and Francesco arrived at his house after the picnic. She thought nothing more about the man from the park. He wasn't anyone important, surely. She was just jumpy and overreacting. People stared at her all the time, but that didn't mean they were her kidnapper. She was imagining things again. He was long gone, and now she planned to enjoy her time with Francesco.

She turned to Francesco as he guided her towards his bed. "Are you really sure about this, Elena? We can still wait, you know."

Elena nodded. "I am so ready for this."

Gently he unbuttoned her blouse and trailed his hands over her breasts. With one hand, he unclipped her bra and it fell to the ground. He leaned in and sucked her nipples until they were erect, then unzipped her skirt, letting it fall to the floor. He laid her gently on the bed and undressed himself as Elena watched him do a sexy striptease. She felt hot and aroused all over, and had to restrain herself from touching him.

He lay on top of her naked and peeled off her underpants. His mouth kissed her hard on the lips and his hands moved down to her breasts, down to her navel, and in between her thighs. His hands explored her gently, and Elena leaned in closer and kissed him around his throat, enjoying the sounds of his desire.

Elena could barely speak. "Make love to me."

Francesco smiled and fixed his gaze on her. His lips explored her own and his tongue danced with hers as he continued to tease her wetness with his fingers. Elena moaned.

He stopped teasing her. "I think you're ready. Are you okay for me to go on?"

Elena nodded, too aroused for words.

He gently guided his penis into her and together they moved in a beautiful rhythm. Elena felt a mixture of pain and more pleasure, savouring the upcoming climax. Their bodies moved in unison until Francesco and Elena both screamed out in blissful pleasure. Then they held each other in silence.

Was it even possible to love someone so much, yet feel scared of losing them? She was lost in her imagination all over again. Why was she thinking the worst, even in the midst of something so blissful?

CHAPTER 39
CHANGE IN DYNAMIC

The next morning, Elena opened her eyes and lifted up her arms for a stretch. She turned to her side and watched Francesco snore lightly beside her. He was a vision without any clothes on, his tanned chest bare and rugged-looking. He had finally become hers.

Elena lifted the blankets off her and tip-toed to the bathroom, careful to make the least amount of noise possible. She closed the door behind her, found a towel in a low-down cupboard, then turned on the faucet. She was already naked, so she headed into the shower and enjoyed the warm spray tingling her skin. Elena flashed back to Francesco's magic hands and how he had savoured her. He was experienced yet gentle, and it warmed her heart. As her mind imagined last night's scenario, she felt two hands pressing into her back.

"Hi there, gorgeous. Why are you showering without me?"

Elena turned around. Francesco's hands fell to her breasts. He was squeezing them, then placed one nipple in his mouth. She was instantly aroused. "I didn't want to wake you."

He cupped her buttocks and pressed her hard against him. Then he moved her back against the shower screen, lifted up her arms, and landed kisses from her chest down to her navel. He looked up at her and fixed his gaze on her. "I don't think I can get enough of you, Elena. You draw me in like a magnet."

Elena's breathing turned rapid. She watched Francesco's hungry eyes.

Francesco smiled then leaned into her pelvis. "I love it when you have that desire in your eyes. It is so sexy." He kissed her deeply as he caressed her rear. Elena moaned and closed her eyes, enjoying the hot sensation. He probed into her wetness and she felt his stubble rubbing against her cheeks as he explored her mouth even deeper and faster.

His mouth tantalised her. His fingers kept arousing her until she could no longer hold back the explosion. He lifted his head and faced her, his lips ravaging her further. He pulled up her leg and touched her sticky wetness with his penis.

He guided his penis into her and entered her until they both cried out in a climax. Elena opened her eyes, wrapping her arms tightly around Francesco. He kissed her around her neck and began soaping her body. She reciprocated until they were both cleansed.

Elena stepped out of the shower followed by Francesco. "I need to get to school. Can you give me a lift?"

"Sure. We'll get dressed, have some breakfast, then I'll take you." He slapped her on her bottom. "You are gorgeous, you know that." He pushed her across the bed and lay on top of her. His lips explored hers and his tongue delved deeply. "We have time for another round, don't we?"

Elena pushed off him. "No, I have to get dressed."

"Okay, okay, but I'm hoping you'll spend most nights with me."

She shrugged. "I'll need to talk to Nunziata. It's just that I don't want my parents finding out about this."

Francesco nodded. His phone rang in his kitchen. "Hold that thought." He rushed over to the phone and picked it up.

Elena watched him from the bedroom as she was buttoning up her blouse. Francesco was whispering over the phone. *Who was it?*

A few minutes later he returned, but his eyes had darkened and his mood was sombre.

"Are you okay?"

"Hmmm."

He avoided eye contact and dressed in silence. He sighed several times but failed to say anything once he was ready to leave. Elena couldn't let it go. The dynamic had changed.

"Who was that on the phone?"

Francesco stared for a moment before responding. "My father."

"So why has your mood changed? Did he give you bad news?"

He grabbed his car keys from the bedside table and headed to the living area. He seemed to have forgotten breakfast as he pulled her by the hand and led her outside.

Elena held out a hand. "What is going on? We're not leaving here until you tell me."

124

Francesco watched her briefly then locked the door behind them. "Nothing. My father and I don't get along. That's all. He just rubs me the wrong way. Can we go now?"

Elena wasn't buying it. Something more was going on. He was hiding something. This wasn't a good start to their relationship, but she'd give him time. It couldn't be that bad.

CHAPTER 40
BETRAYAL

Elena's gaze fixed on Valentina as she lectured on the theory of designers. "Armani is starting to revolutionise menswear. He's looking at creating a type of jacket that has both comfort and style, as if you're wearing a comfortable jumper. He is pure genius." She paused. "Now with the beginning of your own collection, you might be inspired by Giorgio Armani or potentially Gianni Versace. Last year, he designed instant summer wear which earned him huge popularity in Milan. He then went on to design Florentine Flowers' autumn and winter collections. Truly inspirational. You might choose to go with ready-to wear clothing or haute couture. Maybe even mass market designs. Totally your choice. Now get to work people."

Elena bowed her head and took out her pencil and notepad. She sketched out a design of ready-to-wear clothing. She wanted to design clothing that was expensive, yet not custom-made. She wanted to take a lot of care in the selection and design of the fabric. People tended to appreciate the cut of these designs and would pay a lot of money to simply get the style between haute couture and mass market designs. She had no desire to design mass market as that didn't allow her to showcase her true skills in fashion design. She wanted style, elegance, and richness in her design; one that would eventually scream Elena Allegro. No one else would be Elena Allegro.

She took a breath and looked around the classroom at the hubbub of activity. Isabella was cutting up fabric, Angelo was using a muslin and draped a partial piece of a dress over it, and others sketched, or huddled in a group to share ideas. Others selected fabric from an elongated table along the back of the room.

Valentina circulated the room and offered ideas. She leaned in towards a sketch of a design of Angelo's and shook her head. "This is amateurish, Angelo. You need to look at how this type of cut doesn't flatter the figure. If you're going to design for a woman you need to think like a woman. Get rid of this muslin until you get the design right."

Angelo blushed. He turned to Elena and forced a smirk. Then he bowed his head and dug his pencil deeply into the sketch pad.

Isabella leaned in close to Elena. "What do you think of my designs, Elena? Do you think she'll like them?"

Elena flipped the page to look at a few of Isabella's designs, which featured belted dresses and a mini-skirt. She had a talent and an eye for detail but obviously needed more confidence. "These are amazing. She'll love them, don't worry." She fingered the thickness of the fabric. "But I would go with a softer and thinner fabric for the dress if it's for the summer season. This is more of a winter fabric."

Isabella nodded. "Of course. I think you're right. I'll go to the fabric table." She walked away then Elena returned to her designs. She looked up and felt eyes boring into her. Angelo was glaring as if she'd done something wrong. What was his problem?

***

That evening, Elena had a quick discussion with Nunziata about staying over at Isabella's place for a few nights. She made the excuse of having to work on their designs together for the upcoming fashion collections. Elena hated lying, but for now she had no choice. It was the only way she could be with Francesco. Nunziata would most likely get back to Papa and she'd be sent back to Laurino. She couldn't risk her relationship like that.

She hopped on the bus and made her way to Francesco's house. He'd put a note in her bag telling her to drop by tonight, but she wondered why he didn't tell her in person after he'd dropped her off at school that morning.

Elena brushed off her thoughts as her stomach tingled with anticipation at seeing Francesco again. She missed him during the day and hoped he was in a better mood.

The bus stopped a short way from his house, so she got off and did a little jig as she walked several blocks to his house. She noticed an unfamiliar Fiat parked near Francesco's car and wondered if he had a visitor. Maybe his father or a family member was visiting, or maybe it was one of his friends.

Elena hesitated at the door for a moment, pondering whether he would want to see her if he had a visitor. No one but they knew about their relationship as they wanted to take it slow, but what if she was making a mistake? What if he'd be annoyed with her for just dropping by? That was ludicrous. He had sent her that note and said he wanted to be with her most nights. Surely, she had every right to knock on his door?

Elena knocked and found that the door was slightly ajar. She pushed it open and walked into the foyer in silence. "Francesco. It's me." Not a sound.

She made her way into the kitchen and found dirty dishes in the sink. Two glasses lay on the bench and one of them had a lipstick mark at the rim. Elena froze. Who was he having a drink with? She didn't drink anything with him last night, so it had to be his visitor, but there were no voices nearby. It was silent throughout the house.

Elena headed towards the bathroom, but it was empty. She sneaked towards his bedroom with a sinking feeling in her stomach. She felt uneasy but wasn't sure why. Francesco had invited her, but she felt like she was intruding. Her feet stood frozen outside his door but she heard nothing behind the closed door. Gently, she pushed open the door. Then her feet froze and her vision blurred.

What flashed before her was a woman with bleached-blonde hair, the brightest red lips, and biggest cleavage she had ever seen. She was lying on top of Francesco's bare chest with her eyes closed. Francesco was asleep. Sitting on top of his bedside table was a packet of condoms.

Elena's chest felt empty of any emotion. She was standing in a haze, unable to process the scene before her. It had to be a dream. A dream. Francesco would never cheat on her with this woman. But if that was true, why were they in bed together? Of course they had slept together. It was obvious.

She took a calming breath, even as tears streamed down her cheeks. Putting one foot in front of the other, Elena trudged out of the house and walked aimlessly until she found an empty bench. Her heart was broken. Her life with him was over. She sat on the bench with her face in her hands and wept for a long time.

CHAPTER 41
LOST CONNECTION

When she'd cried herself empty, Elena wiped her eyes and forced herself to think the situation through. She wondered why Francesco had invited her over when he had another woman in his bed. Did he want to hurt her on purpose? Did he plan on her finding out? He'd told her he cared deeply about her, but that was obviously a ruse to get her in his bed. He'd made her fall in love with him and once she did, he betrayed her.

Maybe this was his way of breaking up with her. A way for her to break up with him rather than the other way around. *The bastard!* She'd trusted him with her heart and body, and now he treated her like discarded rubbish. She'd wasted her virginity on a user; a man with no morals; no honour; and no human decency.

A sound in the distance made her turn. Was there someone watching her behind the tree? She could've sworn she heard a rustle of leaves but then again, she wasn't in the right headspace. Probably imagining things again.

Elena would never believe in anyone in the same way again. She was doomed. How could she trust a man again, and how could she continue working with him? She would quit her job and find something else. She had sales experience. She'd make it easy for him, but first she planned on giving him a piece of her mind once he was alert and awake. Maybe those phone calls he was getting weren't from his father. Maybe they were from this other woman. Nunziata did tell her not to trust him. That he had a way of charming women and hurting them. Why didn't she listen? How could she have been so stupid? So naive? He hadn't changed at all over the years. Never again.

***

He hunched behind the tree, wondering if Elena had spotted him. When he peered past the tree, she was seemingly caught up in her own world again. Wiping away her tears, staring out at nothing in particular, and sitting as frozen as a statue, she was deeply wounded. He wondered if she would ever move from that bench. Not that he blamed her, but his clever plan had worked. She was as despondent as ever, and not likely to forgive Francesco for the feigned indiscretion. Now maybe she would leave Milan and realise that this wasn't the right place for her. This was his domain, and she had no right to be in his own home city when she'd done enough.

Besides, she was too young and too inexperienced for this kind of world.

He smiled to himself and ignored the slight tightness in his chest. He looked over at her again, and felt his heart almost pull. That was ridiculous. He shouldn't be feeling sorry for her. He did what he had to do, and he hoped his plan had worked. She was a liability in his life and needed to leave Milan. She'd never earned her right to live and study here. It was time for her to return to her family and fulfil her farm duties. In time, she would forget Francesco and marry someone else. No need for her to have a career when a woman's place was in the home. She could use this time in Milan as a learning experience. If his plan didn't work, he'd have to resort to tougher measures. The tightness in his chest surfaced again.

CHAPTER 42
RELENTLESS

The next morning, Elena flinched at the sound of a door knock as she was filing away her portfolio collection of designs into a large plastic bag. She set it aside in a corner of her bedroom and headed over to the front door. Swinging open the door, she drew back at the sight of Francesco, his hands drawn through his hair, his face pale, with dark circles under his eyes. He managed a smile that didn't touch the guilt in his eyes.

"Can I come in?"

Elena shook her head. "Please leave. I have to get to class soon or I'll be late."

"But you're not due in for another hour. We have time." He leaned in to kiss her, but she moved back. "What's wrong?"

As if the bastard didn't know. Now he was pretending to be all innocent. More lies! How could she ever think he was this sweet, caring guy when all along he'd manipulated her into his bed? "As if you don't know what's wrong. Don't act there all innocent."

She gave the door a hard shove, but he held it open with his feet. "No, we're going to talk about this. Either let me in or let's talk outside. Is Nunziata home?"

"No, you're lucky she's not here or she'd surely kick you out."

Elena swung the door open wider and Francesco entered and headed to the couch. He sat on the edge, his hands fidgeting in his lap. His strong gaze on her was unnerving, and he waited for her to sit in the armchair opposite.

She perched on the edge and leaned forward. "So you're telling me you don't know what's wrong? Really?"

He rubbed his face and closed his eyes for a moment as if processing her words. He stared out the window, avoiding her eyes. As he turned back to her, he said, "I woke up this morning with the biggest headache, but I don't know why. I think something happened last night, but I can't remember. It's like I've got this huge hangover, but I don't know how. I don't remember going out last night or anything. It's all a blur. Did I see you last night?"

Elena was impressed with his act. Really impressed. She took a calming breath and said, "I got a note from you to meet you at your house, but when I got there—when I got there—" She fought back tears and soldiered on. "You were in bed with another woman. You were asleep and so was the woman. I just ran out."

Francesco's eyes widened but he said nothing. He rose from the couch and paced up and down the floor. He rubbed his fingers through his hair again and pursed his lips. Turning to Elena, he approached and touched her cheek. It was only guilt he felt, but nothing more, she thought.

"So, you're not going to say anything?" Elena asked.

He shook his head and stared at the floor. "I told you. I don't remember anything from last night. No drinking or drugs, and definitely no woman."

Elena gave a bitter chuckle. "A likely story. Just your way of pretending you're innocent so you can have your fun on the side. You used me for your own plaything and then decided to discard me like dirt. Well, nicely played, Francesco. A nice story of how you can't remember, but I think you had a great time last night, slept with that woman, and drank far too much to remember it."

Francesco knelt on the ground. He tried to take hold of her hand but she moved it out of reach. "You know me. I would never betray you like that. I don't remember anything about a note either. It's all a blur. I should remember in time, but please trust that I would never cheat on you, Elena. I care about you so much!"

"Words are cheap, Francesco. How do you expect me to believe such a fabricated story? If you wanted a cheap thrill in bed, then that's fine. You could've told me from the start that you only wanted sex. I was a virgin and you took that away from me." She looked away, tears streaming down her face.

Francesco leaned in and pulled her close. Elena couldn't help but lean into him, enjoying the warmth of his arms around her. He pulled away from her and kissed her deeply on the mouth. Elena felt herself responding. Then she came to her senses. Quickly, she pulled away and got up to head to the door. "Just go! I can't believe you right now. It hurts to see that woman in my mind. In your bed."

Francesco stilled. "Please believe what I'm saying. I don't remember sleeping with that woman."

"Maybe you don't remember, but you still cheated." She avoided his eyes and waited.

Francesco looked defeated and nodded. He strolled over to the door and walked out towards his car. She closed the door behind him.

A few minutes later, the door opened and Nunziata came inside. "I just saw Francesco sitting in his car. Then he sped off. What happened?"

She watched Elena cry and pulled her into her arms. There was no need for words, but Elena heard Nunziata say to herself, "*The bastard!*"

CHAPTER 43
MEMORY FLASHES

Francesco unlocked the shop door and displayed the open sign. He closed the door and filled the cash register float with notes from a money bag. His fingers shook as he closed the register and stared ahead at nothing in particular. Heading to the staff room, he sat on the chair, bowed his head into his hands, and turned his head from side to side. His chest ached, and his stomach pinched him. Flashes of Elena's stricken face were in the forefront of his mind. Her rejection of him. Her anger and pain that she tried to hide but failed miserably. He couldn't fathom doing such a despicable thing to Elena.

It wasn't in him to cheat on anyone. He'd never done it before with his ex-girlfriends and he would definitely not cheat on Elena. He loved her. She was special and unique. What could possibly have happened last night?

Francesco shifted his mind to a box of new stock sitting near the window. He grabbed a knife and cut open the box, then rummaged through the new summer trends. He dug in deep and found a variety of mini-skirts, jean shorts, sequined singlet tops, pleated dresses, and halter tops. Without a moment's thought, he unpacked the clothing, sorted them by sizes, priced them with his price gun, then hung them onto racks while discarding last season's clothing. In the background, he played upbeat music that shut out the pain he was feeling. He was glad Loredana was taking a few days' leave. She was taking a road trip to another part of Milan with Biagio. They would've left this morning for their trip, which meant he had some time to salvage this mess before they returned.

He ran his fingers over the finest fabrics, his mind turning to Elena. She looked beautiful even in anger. Yet the pain and sadness in her eyes tugged at his heart. Surely, he didn't sleep with anyone because he supposedly drank too much? He didn't even remember going out after working at the store. It had to be a mistake.

The ringing of the door alerted him to a customer. He walked behind the counter and stared at the familiar-looking woman who approached him and laid a new season's dress on the counter. Her hair was greying at the tips, her eyes were dark, and she held a perfect posture for her towering size.

The lady said, "I bought this yesterday before you closed up and noticed that the seam has unstitched. I didn't even see it until today." She sighed. "I paid a lot for this dress, so I'd like another one."

Francesco fingered the gap in the dress then put it aside. He grabbed another dress from the rack and placed it in the proffered bag. "Here you go. This seems to be fine. My apologies."

The woman scanned the stitching which took a number of minutes until she turned to him. "You know, I saw you close up yesterday evening after I came out of the next shop. This woman with blonde hair was watching you, standing by the kerb. She looked a bit strange and lost. I thought you might've known her, but you looked away. Then she continued to stare and walk in your direction. I thought maybe you knew her and she was trying to get your attention."

He shook his head. "No, I don't know any blonde woman. Did you see what she did after that?"

The woman tilted her head, contemplating. "You both turned the corner and I lost sight of both of you." She placed her strap firmly over her shoulder and shrugged. "Anyway, thanks for replacing this. I'll see you next time."

Francesco nodded, lost in his own thoughts. The remainder of the day he was lost in a haze, serving customers, cleaning the staff area, and clearing old stock to make room for new stock in his store room. He felt dust across the shelves containing folded-up clothes, so grabbed the duster and cleaned around the area. As he worked, his mind turned towards this woman who had been seen watching him. Did she somehow follow him home? He closed his eyes and tried to picture the scene in his mind, but it was pointless. He couldn't remember what had happened after getting home from work. He must've had something heavy at home, but he never drank to the point of intoxication. He knew when to stop as, after a few glasses, he no longer enjoyed the drink.

At the end of the day, Francesco took a deep breath, his body inflating. He missed Elena already and had to make her believe that he'd never intentionally be unfaithful to her. She was like a second skin to him, and he didn't want to lose her.

135

Francesco counted the day's takings and inserted them into his money bag. Then he drove home, had a second cleansing shower, and lay down on the couch, closing his eyes. He drifted into sleep, then awoke with a start, the wisps of a dream already beginning to fade. One thing, though, he remembered.

He held an image in his mind of the blonde woman. She had come to his home and given him some story about running away from an abusive boyfriend down the street from his own house. Tears streamed down her face and she seemed be scared for her life. She asked for a glass of water and he had one too, given he'd just returned from a day's work. Then…what happened? It was a blur after that, but he kept closing his eyes and reliving the scene in his mind.

Francesco rose from the couch and wondered whether he'd washed his glasses yesterday. He looked around the kitchen area but there were no glasses. Maybe he washed them yesterday or maybe not.

He reached up for a glass from the cabinet and found a wet glass that hadn't been dried properly. He took a smell of it but couldn't smell anything. Was it possible that this woman had drugged him? He must've turned away. Otherwise how would she put something in his drink?

CHAPTER 44
CONFIDANTES

"What do you mean Francesco cheated on you?" Loredana said.

Elena bowed her head and recounted the details of the last couple of days. She drew her quaking fingers through her hair and fought back tears.

Isabella sat between Elena and Loredana in a cafe close to the institute, having stopped there after class. Loredana had returned from her road trip a day earlier than scheduled so she was able to meet with them on her day off.

Loredana angled her head then took a sip of her aperitivo. She shook her head and looked away for a moment. "He wouldn't do that, at least not intentionally. I mean, he might've been drunk but I'm sure he wouldn't have had sex with that woman."

Isabella leaned forward, her elbows resting on the table with her fists pressed under her chin. "He probably fell asleep before anything could happen."

Elena processed the feedback, wondering if there was a chance he hadn't had sex with the woman. What if he didn't? Would that change anything?

"Earth to Elena. Earth to Elena," said Loredana. "What's going through that head of yours now?"

Elena shrugged. "I don't know. I just feel deeply hurt. I thought he cared about me like I care about him, but he used me. I feel like dirt. I feel worthless and dirty. As if I should've kept my virginity. He took that away from me, and now if Papa ever finds out, he'll kill me. I don't know if I'll ever trust anyone again."

Isabella rose from her seat and gave Elena a brief hug. Tears streamed down her face as she seemed to feel things just as Elena did. She sat back down when Loredana signalled to the waiter for new orders. He came over, and she ordered an espresso while the others ordered a flat white.

"Look; knowing Francesco, he would never cheat on you. There has to be more to the story," Loredana stressed.

Elena was tired of the subject. "Anyway, tell me about Biagio. How is your love life? At least one of us should be happy in that department."

Loredana hesitated. "Fine, I think. But lately he's been a bit distracted. He says it's just work, but I get the feeling it's something more personal."

Elena swallowed. "How is he distracted?"

Loredana tilted her head and sighed. "I don't know. I guess he hasn't wanted to make love for a couple of weeks now, which is unusual for him, seeing as he can't get enough of me. Anyway, we were talking about you, so enough about my love life."

Isabella nodded. "I agree. What are you going to do?"

Elena turned to the waiter who had set down their drinks. She blew over the steaming cup, smelling the aroma of fresh beans. It warmed her heart a little. "I can't trust him. It's over between us."

Loredana lifted up her hand. "Hold on, that's crazy. If you care about him, then you need to give this a chance. If he said he doesn't remember, then he doesn't remember. Francesco doesn't lie."

Isabella nodded. "You both need to sit down and talk this out, Elena. Give your relationship a chance. There has to be a simple explanation."

"How can you explain a woman in a man's bed? Do you think they were playing cards in bed or having a go at Scrabble? Come on. It's obvious what happened. They barely had any clothes on and she was lying on top of him. There's only one explanation for that, and it's not a reasonable one." Elena exhaled, growing tired of the conversation. "I don't want to talk about this anymore. I need time to think, but I can't do it with him around. I'm leaving the store, so I'll be looking for other work. I can't be around him at the moment."

Loredana peered ahead of her. "Speak of the devil."

Elena turned around. Her heart jumped. Francesco had walked in with a smile splashed across his face. His eyes lit up when he spotted Elena and approached.

Elena drew back. "Leave me alone. I don't want to see you."

"But I have news."

Loredana said, "Go on, spill it, man. We don't have all day."

He looked into Elena's eyes, fixated. "I remember exactly what happened. I'm pretty sure I was drugged and now that the drug's worn off, I remember everything."

CHAPTER 45
CLEAR RECALL

Loredana and Isabella abruptly rose from their seats, staring at one other. Elena turned towards them raising her eyebrows. She looked furious, but he couldn't blame her. If she'd done something like that to Francesco, he'd think twice about speaking to her again.

"See you later, Francesco," said Isabella while Loredana nodded in greeting. As they both stepped out of the coffee shop, Elena's eyes roamed the surrounding area as if to avoid the confrontation. She looked gorgeous in a halter top and a fitted mini-skirt, even as she stood up about to leave. Her hair was tied up in a loose bun with tendrils falling down her flushed cheeks. He wanted to wrap his arms around her and never let her go.

"Please don't go, Elena. Just hear me out. I remember everything."

Elena squinted then turned away for a moment. "Fine, but make it quick. I told Nunziata I'd be home for dinner."

"Thanks." He sat down beside her and clasped his hands. Taking a deep breath, he recounted the incident from several days earlier.

***

Francesco had returned home from work and undressed into casual wear. Once he moved into the kitchen to prepare dinner, a knock on the door startled him. He swung open the door and spotted a blonde woman crying. Her mascara was running down her cheeks and her lipstick was smeared down to her chin. She had bruises around the eyes and down her bare arms. The singlet she wore was torn from the top and there was a huge rip in her leather skirt.

"Please help me! My boyfriend's after me and I think this time he'll kill me. He's at my house but I managed to get out for now. He can't find me."

Francesco genuinely felt sorry for her. "I'll call the police."

The woman shook her head. "No, you can't do that. He'll kill me for sure. I need to get away for a while, then once he's gone, I'll leave this godforsaken city."

"So how can I help you?"

She turned to look over her shoulder, then faced him. "Can I stay here for a little while? I'm sure he'll get tired of looking for me. Then he'll leave and I'll be safe again."

Francesco wasn't sure about letting her stay. He wanted to call the police, but she looked frightened and was pretty badly bruised. He decided to let her in, and hoped that she could soon return home. "Okay, come in."

The woman followed him into the kitchen and sat. "Thank you so much. He'll leave soon. Then I'll be able to go back home and leave for good. He'll never find me then."

"Do you have any family who can pick you up?"

She shook her head, her hands shaking and her foot tapping on the floor. "I don't have family in Milan. They're all in a southern village far from here." She coughed and touched her throat. "I really am thirsty. Can I have a glass of water?"

He nodded then grabbed her the glass of water, setting it in front of her.

"So why did you come to me? Do you live close by?"

The woman turned away briefly then flashed him a smile. "I chose the first house I saw that was far enough from my house. I noticed your car outside so I knew someone would be home. I'm sorry, but I was desperate and needed to find some kind of shelter."

"I see," Francesco said.

"How about you join me for a drink?" The woman said. "I hate to drink alone." Francesco smiled. "Okay." He poured himself water and drank some of it down.

"Can I have a damp towel to get rid of this mess on my skin?"

"Sure. I'll be right back."

Francesco returned with a damp towel and cotton wool for her smudged eyes. "Here you go." He watched her wipe the towel over her face then down to her throat and chest, revealing part of her breast. Francesco looked away, hoping she would leave soon. She put down the towel and drank the remainder of her water.

"Aren't you going to finish your drink?"

"Hmmm." He drank then put both glasses in the sink. "So, how long has this boyfriend of yours been hitting you?"

She shrugged. "I've lost count of the years, but I can't take it anymore. I have to leave him this time. Somewhere he'll never find me." She pressed her lips, then rose from her seat. With both arms outstretched, she leaned into Francesco and wrapped her arms around him. He sat stiffly in his chair, feeling uncomfortable with her closeness. She moaned and stroked the back of his head. "You feel so good in my arms."

Francesco cleared his throat, then pushed her off. He moved out of his seat. "Please don't. I have a girlfriend. You need to go now. I'm sure your boyfriend's gone by now." Something was off about this woman, but he couldn't put his finger on it.

She gave him a reassuring smile. "You wouldn't want to feed me to the wolves, would you? I need help."

Francesco suddenly felt light-headed and dizzy. His vision blurred and the room spun around him. The woman drew closer and touched his cheek.

"Are you alright?" she asked.

"No, I don't feel well."

She turned serious. "I'll help you get into bed. Come on." She grabbed him by the hand and pulled him to his bedroom. He tried to push her away, but he lacked the energy and could barely walk. A few steps away from the bed, he fell to the floor and blacked out.

***

Francesco finished his story and waited for Elena's response, his gaze riveted to her face. Elena sat wide-eyed, staring at Francesco. She didn't say a word but bowed her head as if to process his story. Did she believe the story, or did she think he was lying?

"Talk to me, Elena."

"Well, it kind of sounds impossible and ludicrous, but maybe you should go to the police. This woman obviously played you."

His laugh was bitter. "And tell them what? She might've given me the drug, but there's nothing to show for it. She didn't steal anything, and I didn't get attacked. I'm okay now."

"It sounds crazy, but it also sounds like she took advantage of you."

"I know it probably does sound unbelievable, but that's exactly what happened. You have to believe me. This woman played me, but why she did is the big question."

Elena turned away for a moment, but he gave her time to process the story. He knew he was probably asking too much of her, but she had to believe him. She had to.

Elena reached for his hand. "I guess it's no more crazy than me being drugged by a waiter and kept in a cage." She gave him a reassuring smile. "I'm sorry. I should've had faith in you. In us. I should've known you'd never cheat on me."

He nodded. "It's as clear as day. She used me for something, but I don't know what. Nothing was missing in my house, not even money, so I don't know what she wanted."

He leaned in and kissed her on the lips. "You are my light and my joy for getting up in the mornings. I am yours forever, and would never even think about cheating on you. She obviously tried but nothing happened. I was totally out of it, and that's what she wanted."

"Maybe an ex-girlfriend of yours, taking her revenge."

He stroked her shoulder. "No. I treated them all well."

Francesco had an uneasy feeling about the whole situation. First Elena with the stalker and now this incident with the blonde woman. Were the two incidents connected?

CHAPTER 46
REKINDLED RELATIONSHIP

Francesco pushed Elena against the wall of his home and kissed her hard, his tongue exploring hers as if he couldn't get enough of her. His hands trailed against her erect nipples, playing with them and hearing her moan. She drew herself into him with her own kisses against his neck. He ripped off the buttons of her shirt and leaned into her nipple, sucking her breasts. Elena drew her head back and pressed his head into her chest, relishing the arousal between her thighs.

Elena's wetness was out of control and she wanted him to take her there and then, but Francesco had other ideas when he pulled her away from the wall and threw her gently on his bed. He grabbed an ice cube and rubbed it over her breasts, bringing it down to her abdomen, her waist, hips, and in between her thighs. The sensual act made her want him even more. It was surreal. "It's not too cold, is it?"

She shook her head and closed her eyes, enjoying the chilled sensation when his tongue licked the water away from her body. He teased her with his mouth and watched her lick her lips, moaning. She was totally aroused when he probed his finger inside her. "Oh, you are so beautiful. So beautiful."

He lay on top of her and guided himself inside her, moving in rhythm to her own movements. She closed her eyes to enjoy the gentle sensations. His hands held her buttocks and he kissed her hungrily when they climaxed in unison.

Elena and Francesco lay in each other's arms and stayed quiet for a few moments. She thought about their separation and how she struggled being without him. He was a part of her now, and she wanted him to know that.

His fingers played with her nipple and he smiled up at her. "Penny for your thoughts."

Elena shrugged. "I'm so happy being with you. I want you to know that." She looked up at him. "I just found it hard thinking you'd betrayed me that way."

His eyes darkened. "I would never do that to you. Don't you know how much I care about you by now? There's never been anyone like you. You're it for me."

"So what happens once I finish my course here? My parents will probably want me to go home. My papa surely will."

Francesco stroked her hand. "Your parents know that you can't be a fashion designer in Laurino. This is the place you'll find work."

She nodded. "I know that, but my papa's pretty strict. I don't think he was prepared to think that far ahead. He was very strict with Valeria."

"But she's free of him in Australia now, right? With her husband and daughter?"

Elena smiled, a warm feeling permeating her body. She missed her sister, and hopefully one day could visit. She might be able to make enough money to travel to Australia one day.

"She's very happy, but she had to suffer to get that." Elena swallowed. "She lost the love of her life in Italy, and she had a crazed madman after her. Gregorio was totally obsessed with Valeria, to the point that her boyfriend at the time was accidentally pushed into an oncoming car. It was such a tragedy."

Francesco leaned in and wrapped his arms around her. "I'm sorry. Things like that should never happen, but unfortunately they do." He stroked her cheek. "So what happened to this Gregorio?"

"Apparently he's doing well. He's out of prison and has a job, I believe."

"So at least she's free of him too. It turned out well in the end."

She wondered about Gregorio though. He might look good on the surface but what if he wasn't? What if there were still underlying issues that gnawed at him, to the point of taking revenge on Valeria's sister? She wondered if Gregorio was her kidnapper, but that was ridiculous. What reason did he have for wanting her to leave Milan?

CHAPTER 47
THE RISK OF RETURN

Elena pulled tight on her jacket and turned to Francesco who wore a cheeky smile.

"How about round two?" he said.

"You're insatiable. Can't you ever get enough?"

He snuggled up to her and licked her neck. "Never of you." His eyes turned serious. "Do you really have to go? You can stay the night."

She shook her head. "I don't mind catching a taxi, you know. You don't have to drive me. I mean, it's not that dark outside so I can either catch the bus or a taxi."

"No way. I'm driving you. Give me a minute to grab my keys. I can't seem to find them."

Elena yawned and watched him scour his bedroom for his keys. Once he found them resting on the foot of the bed, his phone rang. "You answer that, and I'll just go to the bathroom."

"Alright. I won't be long."

She headed to the bathroom and peered out the open window, feeling the warm, soft breeze. The blue sky was turning grey as if a storm was coming. Hugging her body tight, she relieved herself and moved back into the living area.

Elena heard Francesco's raised voice in the living room. She wondered who he was talking to. Maybe it was his father, the one he said he didn't get along with. Probably just like her papa, who had his own mindset.

Elena stood against the wall and waited for him to finish the conversation. His back was towards her, so he didn't see her in the room. She couldn't disturb him from the call, so she watched and waited, her mind churning at the turn of the conversation.

"What the hell! You have to stop this, Father. I am not spying on Elena for your friend anymore. It's over. She is an adult and doesn't need me to report to you about her. I know she's safe, so let Enzo know that." Silence. "Of course not. She's no more than a friend. I don't feel that way about her. She's just a child compared to me. You know I like older women. She means nothing to me, and I am tired of being Enzo's spy." More silence.

"I am an acquaintance, that's all. She works for me, so you don't need to worry about her. Just let her be. I've had enough of this."

Elena's hands felt numb, her body shaking. She almost fell to the ground but took deep breaths to calm herself down. Francesco didn't really care about her? He used her just to be her papa's spy. She was just a child and a mere acquaintance. What the hell! How could she have been so stupid?

Francesco hung up the phone and turned around. His face went white at the sight of Elena standing before him. *The bastard! Guilty as sin!*

Elena scurried out and heard footsteps behind her. She almost knocked herself against the door but manoeuvred around it.

"Elena. I can explain. Please don't go!"

He grabbed hold of her from behind before she exited the house. *Liar! User!* She pushed herself away and ran like the wind.

Her legs carried her down the footpath, past the towering trees, and towards other houses and people walking the tracks. After a while, she stopped hearing Francesco's ranting and footsteps and heard only quiet. She ran and ran until her legs gave out, and she cried some more under a wilting tree. Bowing her head over her knees, she closed her eyes and gave in to the sadness and pain.

When she composed herself, Elena walked the path back to her house as she had no money for the bus. It took her many hours to get home, but she eventually arrived there, red-eyed and dishevelled.

***

Nunziata opened the door and Elena ran into her arms, crying. "My God, Elena. What happened to you, darling?" Elena shrugged as they entered the house. Nunziata made her a cup of tea with a warm brioche set on a plate, and Elena brought the steaming cup to her mouth, wanting to forget the night ever happened. Looking at the pastry made her sick, so she didn't touch it. Nunziata sighed. "It's about Francesco, isn't it? What's he done now?"

Elena looked down into her cup and felt more tears burn her cheeks. She wiped them away with her hand, her head pounding and dizzy. She just wanted to crawl into bed and hope that what she'd heard was a dream. But it wasn't a dream. It was very real.

She had to get it out of her system, so she vented until she was spent. Nunziata listened without interruption, then gave her a reassuring smile.

"His father is a tough man, so I can understand why he would've said those words. But it doesn't mean they're real."

"They sounded convincing to me. He said it without a doubt."

"He is a man you'd want to convince. Believe me. I have met him, and he can make your papa look like an angel. Your papa was just looking out for you, Elena. A father's love, that's all."

"You warned me about Francesco, and you were right."

Nunziata held on to her hand. "Eat the brioche. Things will look different in the morning. You need time to process this, so don't rush into any decisions. Give it time to settle in your mind. Be patient with this matter."

Elena suddenly felt more hopeful but still hurting. She didn't know whether Francesco was a liar or protecting himself from his father.

"By the way, your mama called. I had to tell her you were with a friend. I don't think she'd appreciate you being at Francesco's house." She took hold of Elena's hand with a dark expression. "You know, you didn't have to lie to me. I understand you'd want to be with Francesco. I think he is a changed man. I've had a few conversations with him at his shop, and he seems a lot more mature and wise than I gave him credit for. I don't believe he's the womaniser he used to be. I really think he's changed, and I can tell he genuinely cares about you."

Elena looked up, ignoring her last comments. She was surprised by the change in her outlook over Francesco. Who would've thought? "So, what did Mama say?"

"She will call you tomorrow, but mentioned something about a Gregorio and how his sister is worried about him for some reason."

Elena's heart beat fast. "Gregorio?"

Nunziata nodded. "She didn't give me any details, but maybe you should ring her tomorrow. Don't let her worry about you."

Elena rose from the table. "I will. Goodnight."

"Goodnight, Elena. Try to get some rest. Things will get better, don't you worry."

Elena wondered whether she should stay in Milan as she walked towards her room. Laurino was looking pretty good right now. But what was going on with Gregorio?

CHAPTER 48
TRUST ISSUES

(June 1973)

The next day, Elena sat with a piece of fabric and created a sample of embroidered designs. She sewed on buttons and sequins and watched as others in the class prepared designs for a collection portfolio. Scents of cinnamon, lavender, musk, and mint surrounded the classroom as most of the students wanted to impress a renowned fashion designer who was visiting later that day. Elena had other things on her mind. The designer planned to lecture on the history of art and design as the college year was coming to a close.

Her feet felt like they were sinking into the floor as her mind wandered. She took notes from the whiteboard but kept returning to her thoughts. She was going to have to go back to Francesco's apartment. Not that she ever wanted to see him again, but in her haste, she'd left her bag on his kitchen table. Nunziata had lent her money for the bus, but she had to get her bag back.

Her fingers eyed the needle as she pushed it through the fabric of a knitted top she'd designed for her portfolio collection. The material ripped at its seams, and she stumbled with her needle, pricking her finger. Blood poured onto the fabric and Elena cursed under her breath. She dabbed on the fabric with tissue, but it smeared and made it look worse. Sighing, Elena shook her head and cowered, hoping that Valentina wouldn't notice. Most likely she'd have to finish her decorative work at home and wash the fabric.

She looked up, noticing Angelo staring with wide eyes. *What was his problem?* He turned to the front to watch Isabella approach the teacher about her own design. Then his gaze swept past her and to the door. A figure approached the front, and her chest tightened. Francesco uttered a few words to Valentina who called out to her.

"You have a visitor. You can take a five-minute break, Elena, but that's all. We have the guest speaker arriving shortly."

Elena ignored her fluttering heart and flushed face as Francesco fixed his gaze on her, unmoving. Finally, he walked outside the classroom and she followed him. Her legs felt like lead as she swallowed her pride and walked outside. Luckily, nobody was around. She didn't want an audience.

Francesco led her to an empty classroom and shut the door behind him. He handed her the bag she'd left behind. "I'm so sorry about last night. Please let me explain."

Elena glared at him. "What? How I mean nothing to you, and how I'm too young. That you usually go for older females." She swallowed. "How stupid was I to fall for your damn lies again."

"It wasn't like that. My father; he's difficult. I had to lie to him in order to keep the peace. If this went back to your father, I'd have hell to pay."

She ignored his comment. "And to think that all this time you were spying on me. Checking up on me. I guess our random meeting wasn't so random, was it? You'd probably never hire me in normal circumstances." She looked away. "It was all a lie. Our poor excuse of a relationship is a lie, and don't tell me otherwise." He shook his head and reached out for her hand, but Elena moved herself back against the door. "Don't you touch me! Never again. I'm tired of your lies and your secrecy."

"No, Elena. I love you. My feelings for you were never a lie. Please believe that. I had to do this for both our fathers. Yours wanted to protect you in a strange city, and I fell in love with you. I know I probably should've said something earlier, but I knew you'd react this way. They both put me in an impossible situation. I mean, I never expected to fall hard for you. I was only doing them a favour."

Elena blinked. He loved her? The burst of joy she'd felt at those words seemed almost ludicrous, but it left her no room for doubt. She loved him too. Loved him, but needed time to think this through. Without answering, she headed towards the door.

Francesco pulled her back to him and touched her cheek. "Please don't go. Have dinner with me tonight. We'll talk about this properly. You can't give up on us." He grabbed her hand, but she pulled it away and rushed out the door. Instead of heading to her classroom, she rushed into the nearby ladies' room and cried in one of the cubicles. She smeared her eyeliner as the tears refused to stop, then bowed her head and rested her forehead against her hands.

When she thought enough time had passed, she walked out and headed back to her classroom. On her way over there, Angelo approached and smiled.

"Valentina was wondering where you were, so I offered to come find you."

She rubbed her eyes and took a calming breath. "I'm fine. Let's go."

He stood a bit too close to her and leaned in. "No you're not. You've been crying." His nostrils flared. "What did that bastard do? I'll go teach him a lesson."

"Nothing. Just leave it alone. We need to get back."

He held her back by grabbing onto her shoulders. His face neared hers. "If I was your boyfriend, I would never hurt you like that. I don't think he appreciates you the way I appreciate you."

Elena's stomach constricted. She felt suffocated by his minty breath and walked away, but he took her by the hand and pulled her towards him. He neared her and leaned in to kiss her but Elena pulled away just in time. She shook her head and scurried off, hearing his voice behind her.

"But I love you. Don't turn away from me."

Elena turned back just before entering the room, and immediately wished she hadn't. The look in Angelo's eyes was haunting, cold, and fiery. A gut-wrenching pain pinched her stomach. If looks could kill…

CHAPTER 49
PROSPECTIVE SUMMER JOB

Elena walked into one of the well-known pubs in the Isola area of Milan, smelling the stench of sweat, beer, and spices. The hubbub of activity sent her heart racing with the sections of tables amidst an interior garden. Glass windows on one side of the pub emitted light inside, and the sticky floor was evidence of more than one drink being spilled. Steel bars lined the walls, hanging plants ran down the other side of the walls, and a cross-section of bars ran underneath a glass ceiling.

Elena heard the laughter, the banter, and saw the stern expressions of young couples trying to have a conversation among the clutter of noise. Why did she wish that Francesco was here with her? She had to get him out of her mind.

Elena turned to her companions, Loredana and Biagio, who chose a table at the far end of the pub. They settled in their seats and picked up the drinks and snacks menu.

"What's on order, ladies?"

Elena shrugged. "Just water for me."

Biagio fixed his gaze on her. "We are in one of the most famous pubs in Milan and you want to have water? Try again."

"Alright I'll have an aperitivo."

He nodded. "That's better." He turned to Loredana. "And you, my love?"

"I'll try this spicy beer. Sounds delicious."

He summoned the waiter, who came immediately.

Biagio placed their orders, including fries, when Elena suddenly realised that there was something familiar about him. His mannerisms reminded her of someone, but she couldn't put her finger on it. She remembered having that same sense the day she met him, but it had come to nothing then, and it would come to nothing now. She brushed away the thought and focused on her present company.

Biagio said, "So, how are things with you and Francesco?"

Loredana drew back and gave him a stern look as if to reprimand him.

Elena ignored it. "I don't know if I can ever forgive him."

Biagio put his hand over his chin as if in deep thought. "Does that mean you're not working at the shop anymore? I mean, don't you need the cash?"

She shrugged, wondering what was with all the questions. "I'll find another job in a shop or somewhere. I'll figure it out."

"You know I'm looking for someone to do some cleaning in my house. My last maid resigned, so I'm looking for someone new."

Loredana shoved him on the shoulder. "Elena's not a cleaner, for Christ's sake, Biagio. She has creative, designer hands."

"It's okay, Loredana. I actually wouldn't mind cleaning."

Biagio's eyes glinted. "Great! Why don't you drop by next week and we'll discuss payment and the hours you're available?"

Elena nodded, excited at the prospect of continuing her cash flow. If she didn't get money, she'd have no choice but to return home. She had to find a way to survive with the day-to-day expenses.

The drinks arrived, then the fries came in a medium-sized bowl. They dug into them, the spicy smell arousing Elena's hunger. They were crispy on the outside and soft on the inside, exactly the way she liked them. As she savoured the taste and let the sauce drip down her chin, she closed her eyes to enjoy the experience. She wiped the sauce away with a serviette when a familiar voice in the distance made her jump. Looking up, Francesco ambled in with two of his friends and an attractive woman who leaned into him as she spoke to him. Her gleaming eyes bored into him as she touched his shoulder and threw her head back in laughter. Francesco moved away from her but she managed to slide near him again.

Francesco and his friends sat opposite them, and when Francesco noticed Elena, his face paled. He nodded with a reassuring smile, his eyes remaining fixed on hers. Elena felt the room closing in around her.

Loredana touched her hand. "Are you okay?"

"I'll just ignore him."

"We can go somewhere else if you like," Biagio said.

"Too late. Looks like he's coming over."

Francesco scurried his way over to their table, greeted them with a nod, then said, "Elena, can we talk outside for a minute?"

Elena stood her ground. "We have nothing to talk about."

"Please. Just hear me out."

Elena stared at the bowl of chips and wanted to crawl under a rock. She loved him but how could she ever trust him? How many times would their relationship be rocky this way? Granted; the woman in his bed wasn't entirely his fault. She had used him for whatever reason, but this current situation meant that he was capable of lying to her about other things. How could she base their relationship on no communication and secrecy?

"You've already said your piece, so go back to your lady."

He turned towards his friends, then looked back at her. "You're jealous!" His eyes gleamed. "She's just one of Luca's friends and likes to flirt. I'm not interested in anyone but you. How can I get you to see that?"

"Just leave. I don't have the energy for this tonight."

Francesco leaned in towards her. "Please, Elena. Don't give up on us."

Biagio rose from his side of the table and held Francesco by his shirt collar. "How many damn times does she have to say no to you? Are you thick or something?"

Francesco's eyes darkened, and his face turned to fury. He grabbed Biagio's hands and pushed him back. Biagio raced towards him again, but Loredana shoved him aside.

"What the hell's got into you, Biagio? Stay out of it."

Biagio stared hard at Francesco, a sudden rage evident in his eyes. What had triggered him this way?

Francesco stalked back to his seat with a shake of his head. He bowed his head and avoided Elena's eyes. He was enraged, but she couldn't blame him. Biagio had acted like a jealous boyfriend. She wondered what his real story was, and what had triggered him into fury.

CHAPTER 50
A CALL TO HOME

Elena relished her Sundays, especially in summer time. When the sun reflected against a glass window it was precious. When the early sunrise led her and Emilio to help out on the farm, she always ended up reading her favourite books while Emilio did all the hard work. She felt guilty about that, but she was young and innocent then. Another time, another place.

She lay in bed and stretched out her arms in a yawn, slowly opening her eyes as she felt the glare against her window. The sounds of chirping crickets and crowing roosters brought out the new morning, and she wanted to relish it but felt a deep hole in her heart. She wanted to get the missing part back.

Feeling the soft sheets over her sweaty body, Elena rose and yawned again. She took a shower then dressed. Walking into the kitchen, she greeted Nunziata.

Nunziata smiled. "Good morning, my dear. Can I make you some eggs?"

"That would be great, thanks."

She nodded, took out two eggs from the fridge, and cracked them into a cast-iron pan. As she was frying the eggs, she turned to Elena. "Did you enjoy your night out?"

Elena lifted a shoulder. She explained the incident with Francesco.

"Look, I agree he should've told you, but like he said, you would've reacted the exact same way. He didn't know he'd fall in love with you when he agreed to help out your father. It was just a coincidence it happened that way. I mean, would you have handled it differently if you had been in his situation?"

"I don't know. Maybe or maybe not."

Nunziata set the eggs onto a plate and carried it over to Elena. Elena suddenly had no appetite, but she would still eat after her effort.

Nunziata set the plate on the table. "Love is about fighting for what you believe. Nothing comes easy, especially relationships. I mean, if you run every time you face hardship, then what does that say about your commitment?"

Elena grabbed bread from the bread basket, sat down, and dipped it into her eggs while Nunziata watched her. She had the feeling that Francesco had grown on Nunziata, but Elena still wasn't sure she could forgive him. On the other hand, maybe she was giving up too easily, and without a fight.

***

Elena grabbed the telephone and rang her mother in Laurino. She took a deep breath. It had been a while since she'd spoken to her mother, so it was time.

Answering after a few rings, her mother shouted, "Oh, Elena. How I've missed you so much. How are you, my darling?"

"I'm doing well. I've just finished the first year of my design course, so I have two more years to go." Silence. "Mama? Are you there?"

"Of course I'm here. I just miss you, that's all. Will you come visit soon?"

"I don't know. I'm not exactly feeling friendly towards Papa these days."

"What do you mean?"

"Oh, come on, Mama. I'm sure you know what Papa did."

"I haven't the faintest."

Maybe Mama didn't know. "He got this guy in Milan to spy on me while pretending that he needed someone to work in his clothing store."

"Oh, darling, I'm sorry, but you know how your father is. He's very protective. You have to know that it was his way of showing you he loves you and wants you to be safe. He trusted this boy, no doubt."

"He's friends with his papa."

"Who is it?"

"Francesco's father, but I don't know his name." Silence. "Mama?"

"Yes, I know him. If you thought your father was controlling, then you'd be very surprised by Vito. He is not a very nice man, my darling. He always has to step on people's toes to get what he wants. Your father is tame compared to him. Luckily, Francesco is a nice boy. Very different from his papa."

She ignored her mother's last comment. "I don't care. Papa should've trusted me."

"Oh, Elena. Please don't resent him. A daughter must love and respect her papa. Don't be like Giovanna's children who had resented her for a long time. I mean, even now, Daniela told me that her brothers Aldo, and even Gregorio, didn't like how Giovanna gave you part of their inheritance. They still refuse to accept it."

Elena had no idea. "And Daniela? How does she feel?"

"She's okay with it. I mean, she plans to move out of Laurino to start her own business with the money. She's a hard worker, not like Aldo who seems to want things easily and for free. But don't you worry about him. He'll eventually accept it. Gregorio too."

Elena felt a tightness in her throat. "After all the horrible things Gregorio did to Valeria, he's now sulking about the inheritance? He's truly unbelievable."

"I think Gregorio is easier to influence regarding the inheritance, according to Daniela. I don't know whether Aldo can be as easily influenced."

"So where are Aldo and Gregorio now?"

"I don't know. Daniela's lost touch with Aldo as he hasn't returned any of her calls. As for Gregorio, I never asked Daniela where he's staying."

Elena waited for more. "Anyway, Elena. Will you talk to your papa? I'll get him right now."

She swallowed. "Okay, I guess I'll speak to him." She would give him a piece of her mind. Although as she thought about her father trying to protect her, her mind flashed to Aldo and even Gregorio, who were both strange and unusual men. She wondered where both of them were living now, and if either of the brothers owned a warehouse with a human-sized cage.

CHAPTER 51
A COMPANION

Elena bowed her head as she walked along the shopping street of Corsa di Porta Ticinese, feeling the cracked concrete and gaps underneath her feet. She passed by vintage clothing stores, street wear, original accessories stores, record stores, chic style dress stores, and niche brand stores. She browsed in a few of these stores, but only to take her mind off Francesco. He was constantly showing up in her head, but she wanted a distraction by immersing herself in fashion and accessories. Potentially, it gave her further ideas for designs once she started her new school year.

Elena had considered going home for the summer, but she couldn't afford the cost of travel. Her funds were low after leaving the store, and she wouldn't start her cleaning job until after next week. Maybe she would try going home in the middle of her second year; even for a weekend, but she would save up for it.

Stepping into an ice-cream shop, Elena ordered a crepe and sat outside to eat it. She relished the juice and texture of the berries and cream, enjoying the fresh flavour and sweetness. She put aside her plate and stared down at her gold bracelet with its diamonds and charms, and her name engraved on it. The piece of jewellery made her feel comforted, safe even, but she might have to return it. She hated to give it up, but if they couldn't be together, what was the point of keeping it?

With her head down, Elena felt a presence. She lifted up her head and spotted Angelo, who had a concerned look on his face. He invited himself to sit down opposite her and panted as if he'd run a marathon.

"What are you doing here?"

He turned around as if expecting to see someone, then he turned back. "I swear that someone was following you. Someone wearing a hood, someone very bulky and tall. I tried to chase after him, but he got away."

Elena swallowed, wondering why he'd make up such stories. "Why are you lying to me? Is this an excuse to sit near me?"

Angelo drew his hands together. He stared into his stubby fingers, playing with his nails. "You think so little of me, don't you?"

Elena wanted to laugh. He'd done nothing to deserve anything more, and yet he acted genuinely. Maybe he wanted to believe what he was saying.

She stared into the distance but didn't see anyone wearing a hooded jacket. It had to be his imagination. The only problem was that she'd never told Angelo that her kidnapper wore a hooded jacket or that he was tall. Although what if it was Angelo who was her kidnapper, pretending to see a man that way when it was really him? He might've disguised himself, making himself appear taller and bulkier.

"Why would a man be following me?"

He shrugged. "I don't know. Maybe you've got another admirer apart from me and Francesco." Elena didn't respond. "So how is your boyfriend anyway?"

Elena turned away. "None of your business."

His eyes showed a hint of darkness, but he hid it. "Are you okay?"

"I'll live."

He rubbed his hands together, his eyes roaming until settling his gaze on her. "So will there ever be a chance for us, Elena? I still want you."

Oh, when would this end? He was stubborn and refused to give up on her. She started to wonder again if maybe he was the man who had been terrorising her, but then again, the kidnapper wanted to run her out of town. It couldn't be Angelo.

She changed the subject. "So how are you spending your summer?"

"Next week I'll be visiting an aunt who lives in Tuscany. Lots of organic food and helping out on the farm. It's quite a beautiful place, actually. You should come."

Elena sighed. "I don't think so. I'll be working over the summer doing some house cleaning. I need the extra cash."

Angelo tilted his head. "Whose house are you cleaning?"

"Just the boyfriend of a friend of mine. I'm meeting with him next week."

He squinted as if processing the information. "Why would he hire you to clean when some cleaners in Italy charge very cheaply for their cleaning services? He'll probably have to pay you more, given you're a friend of his girlfriend."

"I guess he's being generous and wants to help."

"Hmmm, a bit of a strange offer, especially if he lives alone."

What business was it of Angelo's to interfere? Biagio was simply being nice and wanted to give her cash. It had to work out for both of them in the end.

CHAPTER 52
LETTERS

The next day, Loredana sat in a cafe with Isabella reading aloud a typed letter written by Elena.

I'm sorry to do this in a letter but I had to leave Milan and go back home. The problems with Francesco upset me, the course was not satisfying me any longer, and the money issues have all given me reason to return to Laurino. An emergency back home also gave me a stronger reason to return, and I no longer have a life here. I will miss you all, and will make contact with you once I have settled back home.

> *Love,*
> *Elena*

"My God! Why would she leave without telling us in person? It's so cold and so unlike her," Isabella said. She stared at the letter again, shaking her head, tears streaming down her cheeks. Loredana stroked her hand and gave her a reassuring smile. The poor girl looked devastated. Elena did tell her that Isabella was lonely before meeting her, and now she'd be lost without her friend.

"It just doesn't make sense. I mean, next week she was going to see Biagio for a cleaning job at his home. She needed the money so that would've helped. She also loved her studies and would never leave without saying goodbye in person. Something more is going on, and I'm going to find out," Loredana said.

Isabella wiped her flushed cheeks, her eyes darkening. "How?"

"Well, I'll speak to Nunziata then I'll speak to her family. See what's going on with her."

Isabella peered into the distance. "But what if she's gone somewhere else? Contacting her family might worry them if she's not there."

"Would she have lied about returning home, do you think?"

Isabella shrugged. "From my understanding, she was upset with her father and hated working on the farm. I don't think she'd want a life back there even if money was tight. You know

Elena. She always fights for what she believes in. I refuse to believe otherwise."

"Hmmm," was all Loredana said.

"Let's go and see Nunziata. I'm sure she'll be home."

Isabella nodded and followed her outside the cafe towards the bus stop. Their trip was uneventful, and it didn't take them long to reach her house.

Stepping off the bus, Loredana knocked on the door while Isabella stood awkwardly beside her. The door swung open, and Nunziata's eyes looked red and swollen. She angled her head.

"Well, this is a surprise. What can I do for you?"

Loredana took a step. "Are you okay?"

Nunziata opened the door wider and invited them in. She led them to the couch and sat cross-armed while the girls sat around her. She grabbed a piece of shrivelled paper from the arm of the couch and handed it to Loredana. "Read this."

Loredana scanned the letter and lost all breath. "So she didn't even say goodbye to you? I mean, you live with her."

Nunziata nodded. "I thought we had a close relationship but obviously I was wrong." She held her head low as if it weighed heavily on her. Loredana didn't know what to say or how to console her, but she was going to find out why Elena had done this to all of them. How could she treat them like they'd meant nothing to her? She thought Elena was a true friend but not by the way she wrote these letters. It was cruel, almost evil.

Isabella broke into their thoughts. "She wouldn't do this without a very good reason. There has to be something else going on. Maybe an emergency in the family, one she couldn't tell anyone about. Maybe someone died. Who knows? It could be anything, so let's not speculate. Let's get to the truth."

Loredana looked up. "And how do we do that?"

"Well, maybe Francesco knows where she is or maybe your boyfriend has contacts? We can ask around."

Nunziata broke out of her trance. "Do you really think that some kind of emergency might've driven her home?"

"It's possible," said Isabella. "She wouldn't abandon us like this. It's not like Elena, so something powerful had to have driven her away."

"Yes, that has to be it," Nunziata said with a hopeful expression on her face.

163

Loredana wouldn't give up on this. She'd speak to Francesco and Biagio and search for her. If there was a family emergency, then surely she'd be home.

CHAPTER 53
HEARTBREAK

Loredana smiled at Biagio as he wrapped his strong arms around her, stroking her hair. They seated themselves in a cafe, the strange muffles of people pressing hard into her head. A migraine hit her, so she massaged her temples and briefly closed her eyes, thinking about Elena. Something wasn't right. An uneasiness settled over her chest as she swallowed and stared at her boyfriend, who was fixated on the menu. In spite of smelling the wafts of spices, sauces, and other cooking smells, Loredana was numb to anything around her. Nothing felt the same since Elena left, and she missed her terribly.

Biagio placed their order of cappuccinos with the approaching waiter who disappeared as quickly as he arrived. He turned to Loredana. "What's your plan with Elena?"

Loredana shrugged. "I don't know. I mean, I spoke to Nunziata and I almost rang her family's neighbour as her parents don't have a phone."

His eyes darkened. "Why didn't you? Ring the neighbour?"

"Well, it's only been a day or so. I'll give it another day and then I'll call. She might ring us in the meantime."

Biagio squinted, placing his hand over his mouth and peering at patrons entering the busy cafe. He watched her thoughtfully as if measuring his next words. "Maybe give it a week or so. If there is an emergency, let her deal with it. Give her time to settle, and all that. I'm sure she's fine."

Loredana pondered his words. Maybe he was right. But what if he was wrong? What if Elena was in some kind of trouble? She thought back to the person terrorising her and how she'd been kidnapped. Was the guy back? Should she approach the police?

"It's just that she wouldn't say goodbye to us in a letter. We were all very close. I mean, she lives with Nunziata and didn't even say a proper goodbye to her. She wasn't the type of person who didn't care. She had heart and soul and would never do this to us."

Biagio turned to the waiter who set down their hot drinks and left with a smile. "I think sometimes extreme circumstances force people to behave in ways they wouldn't normally behave."

Loredana's chest burned. "What the hell does that mean?"

Biagio hesitated. "Just that. I'm sure she had an emergency that topped anything else. She would've been too preoccupied with the emergency."

Loredana crossed her arms, staring at her drink. Suddenly she wanted to give back the drink, and felt a sour taste in her mouth. "Are you going to help me or not? All I hear are your damn excuses."

"I just want you to be realistic. Face possible facts."

She sighed. "You don't know Elena the way I do, so don't judge her."

Biagio remained silent as he sipped on his drink. Loredana drank her cappuccino down, allowing the heat to burn her throat as she fought back tears. She wouldn't cry for Elena. She had to be okay. The kidnapper didn't take her. He was long gone, surely?

Biagio set down his mug and took her hand across the table. "I'm sorry, Loredana. I can go home and make a few calls around the village. I know a few people in Laurino. Being a small village, I'm sure they'd know what's going on with her family."

Loredana's shoulders relaxed. "You're a lifesaver. Can I come with you?"

Biagio gave her a reassuring smile. "No need. I can meet you at your place later."

"Okay. I'll wait for you at home; say about 3.00?"

He nodded. "Sure. That'll work."

After finishing their conversation, Loredana and Biagio went their own ways. The dense heat penetrated Loredana's skin as she fought to breathe in the humidity and brazen wind. The sun's rays pierced her eyes as she rummaged in her handbag for a pair of sunglasses. She put them on and rushed home to complete the accounts for the last month's sales from the fashion boutique. She hated to work on a Sunday, but finances were a necessity, and luckily the shop was doing well.

Francesco wanted to close the store for a few days but Loredana mentioned covering his shifts in the meantime so he could search for Elena. If she was in Laurino, she would be fine. Hopefully, Biagio would get some answers.

CHAPTER 54
ON A MISSION

Francesco gripped the receiver of the phone, sighing heavily. He drew his hands through his hair and swallowed.

"Papa, you cannot tell me you haven't seen her. In her letter she explicitly said that she was going back home. Mentioned some kind of emergency."

Francesco had come clean to his father about his relationship with Elena, and his father wasn't too happy about it. Not that he cared any longer, as it was time to assert some control over his father. He'd never let his father dominate him again.

Elena had brought out a strength in him that he'd never known he had.

His father grunted. "She is not here. Of that I am sure."

"Have you seen her father?"

"Yes, and according to him, Elena was fine in Milan. He'd spoken to her recently and she was good. Now leave it alone. She left you, so just accept it. Be a man. No woman is worth your dignity."

So typical of his father to be emotionless about everything. If this had happened to Francesco's mother, his father wouldn't care.

"And when did you see him last?"

"Yesterday, and Elena wasn't with him. She is not here. How many times do I have to drum that into your brain?"

"I'm worried about her. She wouldn't just leave the way she did. Can you maybe talk to her father about whether he heard from her today? Please, Papa!"

"Fine, but then you will leave it alone. I am sure she will be here soon. She probably stopped by somewhere else first. There is no need to worry her father if she plans on coming to Laurino soon."

Francesco nodded. "Okay, thanks. Please keep me updated."

"Goodbye."

He hung up the phone, bowing his head and covering his face with his hands. Tears streamed down his face as he struggled to breathe. His whole body ached, and his throat felt parched. He headed to the sink and grabbed a glass of water. The water didn't help. Nothing helped. Elena was missing, and she wasn't in Laurino like she said she'd be. So where in the hell was she? She wasn't in Milan, as he'd asked his friends. He even asked the local people in the nearby fashion stores if Elena had come around, but she hadn't. She had vanished like a feather in a strong wind.

He needed to let Loredana and her other friends know that she wasn't in Laurino. He wanted to contact the police, but they were hopeless, and she probably hadn't been missing long enough for them to care. Most likely, they'd say it wasn't suspicious because of the letter, but what if she didn't write that letter? What if something sinister was happening?

***

"My God, no!! She's not in Laurino. Are you sure?" Loredana picked at her skin and cried. She put the coffee cups in the sink and sat back at her kitchen table.

Francesco hugged her. "I'm sorry, but let's hope that she did stop by somewhere else. Then we might hear from her." He pulled apart from her.

"So what now?"

Francesco looked away, thinking. "Well, didn't you say that Biagio was calling some people in Laurino? Maybe she's staying somewhere else. You know how strict her father is, so she probably wants to be on her own for a while. Biagio might get answers." He looked into the distance. "She might've needed a bit of time and space away from me, so she might turn up soon." Though, a part of him didn't really believe she'd left of her own free will.

"Biagio's coming here at 3.00 so I'll find out then."

Francesco peered down at his watch. It was 1.00. "I can't wait that long. I'm going to his place. What's his address?"

"Why don't we wait. It's only a couple more hours."

Francesco clenched his hands. "I cannot wait. I need to make sure she's okay, and if Biagio heard anything I need to know about it. I mean, you left him hours ago so I'm sure he's already called." He went to her front door, not wanting to waste any more time. He had to try every means possible to find Elena. She couldn't simply disappear into thin air.

169

"Okay, I'll come with you. Just let me get my bag."

Francesco ushered Loredana out the door and hurried to his car in a heated frenzy. He drove off without regard to traffic lights. Luckily the traffic was light, but it wouldn't have mattered either way. He was determined to find Elena, and he wouldn't stop until he did. Even if it killed him.

CHAPTER 55
A BRACELET

Loredana knocked on the heavy door, turning to the side to focus on the weed-filled garden and dying flowers. She wondered if Biagio worried about his front garden, as it was so unkempt. Francesco stood beside her and waited in trepidation, fidgeting and breathing heavily.

The door swung open a fraction. Biagio drew back with a frown, then stepped outside and closed the door behind him, forcing them to move back. "What are you doing here? I told you I'd come to your place."

She looked to Francesco, who shook his head. "He wanted to know about your contacts in Laurino and couldn't wait."

Biagio cleared his throat. "Look, I called a few people and they told me she was home with her family. You see. You don't need to worry. They expect she'll be in touch soon."

Francesco leaned in towards him. "That can't be right. My papa just said that Elena wasn't there yesterday, so unless she got there today."

"I guess that must be it. I think they did mention she got there today and that her family was surprised to see her."

Loredana nodded. "Who did you call?"

Biagio played with the skin over his wrist. He turned towards her. "Just friends of the family."

"And what are their names?" Francesco asked.

Biagio hesitated and stared at both of them. "The Cesare family. I don't know them that well, but they live nearby."

"Have they lived there long? I've never heard of them," said Francesco.

He ignored the question. "Listen, Loredana. Do you mind if we don't catch up later? I think I'm coming down with the flu."

Her body twitched. Something wasn't right about Biagio. He spoke in such a rehearsed way, it almost didn't seem real that Elena was back in Laurino. Although if she just arrived, then surely she would call soon. Maybe Loredana's imagination was running away with her.

171

She looked to Francesco. "Okay, we'll leave. I'm sure Elena will call us within the next couple of days. I'll just have to wait."

"That's my girl," Biagio said. He kissed her quickly on the lips and faced his closed door. As he swung it open, she saw something on the floor gleaming. Was that a bracelet? Before she could ask anything, he closed the door with a smile.

Loredana walked along the path and reached Francesco's waiting car. He sat in the driver's seat and started the engine.

"Can you drive around the block and stop on the road? I need to tell you something."

Francesco looked at her strangely then drove for a few minutes. He stopped by the kerb but kept the engine running. "What is it?"

"I saw a bracelet that looked just like the one you gave Elena. It was on the floor not far from the front door."

Francesco's hands tightened around the steering wheel. His lips pursed, and he turned away for a moment. "Do you think it was her bracelet?"

Loredana felt sick to the stomach. "I'm sure it was."

Francesco stared into her eyes. "Tell me truthfully. Is there a possibility he had another woman with him who had a similar bracelet to Elena's?"

Loredana didn't want to think the worst. "The only explanation I can come up with is that Elena was here. Or maybe she still is. I think he was lying."

She noticed Francesco's erratic breathing. He clenched his hands and teeth. His eyes darkened. "Is there any reason why he'd hurt her?"

"I don't know. He's been a bit of a mystery, so I don't know that much about him."

Francesco turned off the motor. "We have to get in there, but maybe we need to do it discreetly. I'll go in the back and somehow try to break in. Does he have a shed or some kind of building outside?"

Loredana nodded. "But surely he wouldn't keep her in there?"

"We have to expect anything at this stage."

"Maybe we should call the police," Loredana said.

"They won't care about a bracelet. They'll say that others have one just like it. Except that her name was engraved on it. That's the difference. We can't be sure she's here. But we need to get you in there. I can go in from the front once you've taken him in the back of the house. You have to distract him."

Loredana breathed in. "Sounds like a plan."

Francesco and Loredana exited the car. They were on their way to get Elena back.

CHAPTER 56
BOUND AND CAPTIVE

Elena bit into her lip and tasted a familiar tang of copper. The rope rubbed against her bound wrists and tore into her skin as she fought back tears and rage. She took calming breaths and peered into the bare room that contained a discoloured dressing table, a dusty bedside table, and an old wrought iron bed to which her hands were tied. She'd tried over the last couple of days to pull hard against the rope in an effort to free herself, but it was too tight. The more she pulled at the rope, the more her skin burned and chafed. It was pointless to try to escape.

The carpeted flooring was worn and ripped in parts of the room, and old newspapers lay scrunched up on the dresser. She angled her head as her eyes discovered a familiar name on the top headline page of the newspaper. Why hadn't she noticed it before? The familiar name. The name that made her queasy. The name she thought she'd never hear again; at least not in this lifetime. Gregorio! It had to be about the time he was arrested for hurting Valeria, but that was about ten years ago. He must've kept the newspapers all these years. Talk about obsession.

So did that mean that Gregorio was holding her captive? It had to be. His way of avenging against Valeria whom he could never have. But why go after her? Because it would hurt Valeria? Valeria was too far away in Australia, so it was easier to target her sister. He must've had this all planned from the beginning. Was he going to kill her? She barely breathed just thinking about her plight, and wondered how she would get out of this situation. Maybe she could move her way to some kind of object that could cut the rope, but there was nothing sharp nearby. She bit into the tight knot, but it was wound too tightly to undo. He must've learned some great survival skills in the woods because he actually knew how to tie a knot.

A scuffling in the distance made her twitch, and she held her breath to keep her captor from hearing her. The sound grew further into the distance, but she could've sworn she heard voices. Someone must've knocked on his front door earlier, but she wasn't sure that was the sound. Luckily, her kidnapper at least fed her and kept her hydrated for now. He didn't ask anything of her and didn't say one word. He'd kept quiet and had continued to wear a clown mask so she couldn't see him. Yet something about his manner was familiar to her. The way he walked and the size of his build. She knew her kidnapper, so it was possible that Gregorio had come to Milan. His build was about the same as her kidnapper's body size. Surely, being in prison would've taught him a lesson but obviously not.

Elena needed a shower. Her hair felt dirty and her skin dry, and she wished for more hydration, but he only saw her a couple of times a day. She had slept most days out of sheer exhaustion, and blinked back tears whenever she tried to sleep during the nights. She wouldn't let this creep take control of her mind and emotions. She refused to succumb to his bullying. She'd find a way to get out of here.

Elena continued to pull at the rope in the hope that she could free herself from the binding, but as she pulled and pulled, her skin chafed and grated. She clenched her teeth to fight off the pain. If she could free herself, the pain would be worth it. So she kept going until no more fight was left in her. Closing her eyes, she laid her head against the back of the bed and felt herself falling asleep for a moment.

That didn't last. The sound of footsteps in the distance jerked her into full wakefulness. They edged closer to her. Then they stopped. Voices grew louder. Then another door slammed from somewhere else. What was going on? Were there people in this house besides her kidnapper? Was he going to get other people to kill her rather than dirty his hands himself? She wouldn't put it past him, seeing as he was too weak to even show his face. He obviously had something to hide but she sensed that Gregorio was her poison and she would need an antidote against it.

The voices grew quiet and silently faded. A door closed, then more footsteps. Sounds of swearing as her kidnapper seemed to be yelling at the top of his voice. Then he screamed, and she wondered if he would take out his rage on her. He kept saying the f-word over and over again until he quieted down. Footsteps approached her room, but she turned away. She didn't have the courage to see who it was. She didn't want to know if he was about to kill her. Thoughts of Francesco, her friends, and her family fell into the forefront of her mind. She would be sorry they would suffer from her death. They would grieve their loss.

The kidnapper was coming for her and he was obviously angry about something. She held her breath and awaited her fate.

CHAPTER 57
CLEAR TRUTHS

Francesco had reached the back door and jiggled with the lock of the screen door until he was able to unlock it. He could now sneak in from the front of the house. It smelled of dirt and rubbish, as if the house hadn't been aired for many weeks. Biagio might not even live here. Maybe this was a front for something more sinister. If he had Elena, Francesco would kill him. Biagio would no longer do this to anyone else. He would no longer roam the earth.

Francesco entered a room but as he looked around and opened wardrobes, he found nothing. The room hadn't been lived in. He made his way to another room, but it was cluttered with boxes and boxes of clothing and work tools. A suitcase lay near the window and held more clothes. A bag of tablets sat on top of the clothing, so he approached and wondered what kinds of tablets these were. Some kind of tranquiliser, no doubt, to subdue his victim so they couldn't fight back.

Francesco had no time to speculate further. He hurried out, careful to avoid Biagio, who was banging pots in his kitchen. Maybe he was cooking dinner, but he was enraged about something as he banged the fridge door and slammed a pan on the table.

Francesco sneaked into another room. Surely this was the last one, as the house wasn't very large. He opened the door, and there she was. Elena had her back to him, her body shaking. He quickly headed towards her and, in a voice breaking with emotion, called her name. She turned around with a quick breath, her eyes dilated.

"Francesco! My God!"

He leaned forward and wrapped his arms around her, stroking her hair and kissing her lips. "Are you alright? Are you alright? You look dehydrated. Let's get you out of here."

Elena nodded. "I'll be fine now that you're here, but we don't have much time."

Quickly he grabbed a small pocket knife from his jeans pocket and cut hard into the rope that tied her to the bed. Soon, Elena's wrists were free. A shadow moved behind him, and she cried out a warning, too late. Her captor dragged Francesco away, landing punch after punch into Francesco's midsection.

Elena scrambled from the bed, flinging away the remnants of the ropes, and rammed Francesco's attacker from behind. He turned around and pushed her to the ground. The mask slipped.

Elena stopped breathing. My God! Biagio? Biagio was her kidnapper? It couldn't possibly be. She could've sworn it was Gregorio. Biagio had never crossed her mind. He was totally in love with Loredana.

He drove a kick into her side that knocked her backward. Her head hit the side of the dresser and a burst of pain shot through her skull. She pushed to her feet on shaking legs, rubbing her head and casting about for a weapon. Biagio slammed a fist into Francesco's jaw, then another. Francesco's eyes looked glazed, but Biagio wouldn't stop. She had to do something. She had to stop him from hurting Francesco, but how? There. In the corner. She grabbed a newspaper, rolled it up tight, then rushed up to him. Swinging back her arm, she shoved the newspaper hard into his eyes. He let go of Francesco, drew back, and groaned in pain.

"You bitch! You'll pay for that."

Elena swung the roll of paper over his head and kicked him in the groin. He fell to the ground, and she pulled Francesco up. His eyes blackened, his nose and mouth bleeding. On unstable legs, she placed one arm around his back and walked him outside the room. She had to call the police.

Her moment was lost when a strong arm wrapped around her waist, shoved Francesco away, and dragged Elena back into the room. Biagio locked the door behind him. Elena turned to her attacker and forced a calm note into her voice.

"Please don't do this. What do you want from me?" She had to get Biagio talking, maybe stall him long enough for Francesco to recover his wits and dial the police or for her to concoct a new plan. She could get out of this.

He held her in a headlock, then pushed her roughly on the bed. "I'm sick of you getting what you want. If you don't leave Milan now, I'm going to kill your whole family, and I mean it this time." Biagio lay on top of her and held his heavy hand against her throat. "You and your whole family make me sick."

Elena struggled to breathe as his hand pressed hard against her throat. Her voice sounded strained. "Why are you doing this? What do you want?"

"You don't know me, do you?" He let go of her throat and her shoulders relaxed.

"Should I?"

He chuckled. "I'm Aldo, Gregorio's brother. My mother gave you an inheritance that was rightfully mine." He shook his head. "Initially I wanted to kill you I was that angry, but then my sister said that you wouldn't spend the money if you lived in Laurino and married a nice village boy. I knew you wouldn't give up the money without a fight, so I came up with a plan to get the money back in Laurino. You don't deserve it. She had no right to give you all that money, taking our share. We earned it, and you didn't." He clenched his fists. "I heard from Daniela who spoke to your mother that you still had quite a bit of money left, seeing as Valeria didn't want her share. Wise woman. So you have a choice. Either you leave Milan or there'll be consequences." He chuckled. "And I want my share when we get back."

His mind was scattered and all over the place, but she guessed it made total sense to him. It was a warped story of a madman. "So you were my kidnapper all along, using Loredana on the way."

He shrugged. "I cared about Loredana, but I had a mission and she wasn't going to get in the way of that."

"If I leave, you expect me to not tell the police about this? You kidnapped me twice."

"I guess if you do, your family will pay."

"And I guess you were the one who set up Francesco with that blonde woman?"

Biagio chuckled. "Easy prey. Francesco was naive enough to let her into his home. Granted, I thought he'd have more brains than that, but the woman was a great actress. The money I paid her to do that job was so worth it."

Elena shook her head. "You're a sick bastard. You need help."

Suddenly the door burst open. Francesco and Loredana pushed Biagio back, and this time the love of her life pounded his fists into Biagio's face. Loredana pulled his hands away.

"That's enough." She pressed the knife in her other hand against Biagio's throat. "I've called the police so if you make one move, I'll cut you like an onion. You've got that, you dirty lying bastard."

Francesco pulled Elena into his arms while Loredana and Biagio sat against the dresser, the knife resting close to his face.

It was finally over!

CHAPTER 58
A NEW PHASE

(Two years later - July, 1975)

Elena brushed a shaky hand through her hair as she stood over a range of designs set on the oak table. Behind her stood a rack of sampled clothing designs for Italian models to try on. Wall to wall displays of textured designs and qualification certificates of her own and those she worked with coloured the white-washed walls. She'd finally made it as an Assistant Designer for one of the most reputable fashion houses in Milan, not long after completing her degree in June. Valentina had recommended her and Isabella to friends of hers, and now they were employed there full time.

Elena and Isabella's roles included researching current trends, coming up with new product ideas, attending fittings, and preparing colour boards. Elena was learning more about the fashion world each day, and absolutely loved her job.

"Have you decided on the designs for the upcoming show?" Isabella said.

Elena shook her head. "Give me a few more minutes, and I'll know then."

Isabella entered the room. "Just research the latest trends and then you'll know. That's part of your job anyway."

Elena turned away from the designs and tinkered with the sample dress on the muslin. She fixed her gaze on her friend and smiled. "This design needs to go to the patternmaker. Can you give the word to Giuseppe?"

"Sure. Anything for my bestie." Isabella rushed away, closing the door behind her.

Elena smiled then grabbed a thick book from the table, flicking through colours to alter some of the current designs her head designer had sketched. She had some input into these designs and wondered about the colours. They didn't work for some designs, but if she softened them to pastel, a few of them would work. She could run it by the designer who could always say no.

Resting the colour book back in its rightful place, she grabbed her notebook from her desk and wrote notes for the designer. She was at lunch at the moment, so she had a bit more time to process things herself. She was dying to create her very first design but all in good time. She rested back against her chair opposite her cluttered desk filled with fabric samples, articles on fashion trends, stationery items, and a phone. Her door swung open, her heart almost leaping into her throat at the figure before her. Francesco!

Francesco strode over to her and leaned in, planting a hungry kiss on her lips. A rush of weakness flooded her legs as she caught her breath, rose, and wrapped her arms around him. Oh, how she missed his touch and sweet kisses. He had been abroad for the past week, opening up a new fashion store in Rome. His business in Milan was booming, so he'd expanded the space by going into partnership with his store neighbour. Then, he'd decided to expand into another city. He had become a famous Italian businessman and she couldn't be prouder.

"I missed you so much, Elena."

"I've missed you too. How was the trip?"

His eyes gleamed as he rested himself on the nearby chair. "They're going to start building the shop in the next couple of weeks. Hopefully the construction won't take too long. I cannot wait."

"You mentioned it taking about six months to build, didn't you?"

He smiled. "Hopefully less than that, but that's the maximum time, otherwise they'll be paying up for the delays. It should all work out." His eyes turned serious. "Anyway, I'd like us to have dinner at my place. Just the two of us. What do you say?"

"Of course, Francesco. But you must be tired."

"Never too tired for my gorgeous girlfriend." He gave a cheeky grin and winked before kissing her briefly and rushing out.

***

Elena and Francesco sipped on wine until he sat her down on the chair in the kitchen. He knelt on one leg, then retrieved a gold box from his pants pocket. Elena gasped and a rush of adrenaline shot through her. Was he doing what she thought he was?

"Elena, I have loved you for just over three years now, and you are the light and brightness in my life. I know we've had our tough times, especially with Biagio." He paused. "Thank God he got justice in prison. He might be out now, but I'll make sure he never hurts you again. He'll have to come through me first. I love you so much." He stared deeply into her eyes and stroked her cheek. "I'll never let anyone hurt you ever again." He took a breath. "Will you marry me?"

Elena lowered herself into his arms and they both sank down to the floor, her body on top of his. "Of course I'll marry you. I love you so much too. I'm yours forever."

Francesco and Elena laughed as they rose from the floor. Footsteps and muffled voices sounded behind her. She turned and smiled at the figures before her. Isabella, Loredana, and Nunziata.

Elena stood cross-armed, shaking her head. "Was this all planned, guys?"

Nunziata wrapped her arms around Elena. "Congratulations, dear. You deserve to be happy." She turned to hug Francesco. Then Loredana made her way in to congratulate them both, followed by Isabella.

"I knew you'd say yes," said Loredana.

"Me too," said Isabella. She turned to Francesco. "For the past week, she couldn't stop talking about you, Francesco. Just don't go away again anytime soon."

Francesco chuckled. "I don't plan to, don't worry." He paused. "Although, pretty soon we'll need to go to Laurino and speak to our families. I'm not looking forward to speaking to my father about the wedding, but he'll have no choice but to come round to our decision. Then I'll pay for the families to come here for the wedding."

Elena winced. "That'll be expensive."

"I'll manage. I mean, my business is doing well, so money's not much of an issue."

She felt tight in her stomach about speaking to her papa but in the end, she was sure he would agree to the marriage. He had softened in his old age, but he had also trusted Francesco enough to have him to spy on her in the beginning.

Loredana lifted up her hands. "Well, this calls for a toast and pizzas. How about you get us a drink, Francesco, and I'll place the order."

"Yes, Captain. At your service," said Francesco as he opened up the fridge.

Elena looked around and took in the laughter and banter of her friends, and knew she was finally home. What was more important than love?

Reviews are gold to authors and allow Lucy to keep writing. If you enjoyed this story, please consider rating and reviewing it on Amazon here: http://mybook.to/Alifebydesign

Go back to the story of Elena's sister, Valeria and her childhood story of the The Italian Family Series in *Dancing In The Rain*: http://mybook.to/dancingintheRain

ABOUT THE AUTHOR

Lucy Appadoo is an author of fiction and nonfiction books. She writes in the genres of romantic suspense/thrillers with significant life themes, contemporary romance, and 20th-century Italian-themed historical family drama/coming of age novels.

Lucy is a qualified counsellor and works as a rehabilitation counsellor for the Australian government. She draws on her life experiences to write inspirational stories about authentic, driven women who manage adversity with strength and heart.

Her favourite authors include Toni Anderson, Kendra Elliot, Blake Pierce, Cheryl Bradshaw, Erica Spindler, Nicholas Sparks, Adriana Trigiani, and James Patterson (to name a few).

Lucy enjoys reading romantic suspense, romance, thrillers, crime novels, family/historical drama, and sagas. She has enjoyed travelling to exotic places such as Madrid, Mauritius, and Italy, and uses her travel experiences to strengthen her creative writing.

Her interests include travel, exercising, journal writing, reading for entertainment or knowledge, meditation, spending time with her husband and two daughters, and socialising with friends and family.

Check out Lucy's website and sign up for a FREE romantic suspense novel here: www.lucyappadooauthor.com.au

ALSO BY LUCY APPADOO

NON-FICTION

Grief & Loss
Moving Beyond Grief - How To Shift From Grief & Loss to
Joy & Peace - http://mybook.to/MovingBeyondGrief

Stress Management & Anxiety
Holistic Spiritual and Mental Health - Building Resilience and
Creativity by Conquering Anxiety and Managing Stress -
http://mybook.to/Holistichealth

Career Guidance
Your Holistic Career Path - Create Career Change, Satisfaction,
and Work/Life Balance -
http://mybook.to/YourHolisticCareerPath

Journal and Record Of Books You've Read (with Quotes)
Readers' Journal - http://mybook.to/ReadersJournal